Alice-Miranda

On Holiday

Jacqueline Harvey

RED FOX

ALICE MIRANDA ON HOLDAY

A RED FOX BOOK 978 1 849 41630 6

Published in Great Britain by Red Fox,
an imprint of Random House Children's Books
A Random House Group Company

Originally published in Australia by Random House Australia in 2010

This edition published 2012

1 3 5 7 9 10 8 6 4 2

Copyright © Jacqueline Harvey, 2010

The Random House Group Limited supports The Forest Stewardship Council (FSC˚), the
leading international forest certification organisation. Our books carrying the FSC label are
printed on FSC˚ certified paper. FSC is the only forest certification scheme endorsed by the
leading environmental organisations, including Greenpeace. Our paper procurement
policy can be found at www.**randomhouse**.co.uk/environment

Red Fox Books are published by Random House Children's Books,
61–63 Uxbridge Road, London W5 5SA

www.**kids**at**randomhouse**.co.uk
www.**totallyrandombooks**.co.uk

Addresses for companies within The Random House Group Limited can
be found at: www.randomhouse.co.uk/offices.htm

THE RANDOM HOUSE GROUP Limited Reg. No. 954009

A CIP catalogue record for this book is available from the British Library.

Printed and bound by CPI Group (UK) ltd, Croydon, CR0 4YY

For Ian,
who makes me laugh

For Sandy,
who loved Alice-Miranda

For Poppy, Nana, Grandad, Joan,
Aunty Joan, Mum, Dad, Sarah, Nat,
Trent, Olivia, Darcy, Flynn and Eden,
just because

Prologue

'Oh my dear man, you're too kind,' Granny Bert blushed, her cheeks matching the colour of her rose-pink teacup.

'No, Mrs Rumble, it is *you* who is too kind. I've so much to do and so little time – your help is humbly appreciated.' The visitor loaded his cake fork with a mouthful of passionfruit sponge.

'Please, call me Albertine,' Granny insisted as she admired the cut of his pinstriped suit.

The small sitting room, already bulging with

1

antique furniture, seemed to overflow with the man's presence.

'Albertine it is, then,' he began. He studied the set of faded plans in front of them. 'Now, what can you tell me? I want to know *all* the secrets.'

As Granny began to reveal the mysteries of Highton Hall, she failed to notice the sickly smile that had spread across her guest's handsome face.

Chapter 1

Alice-Miranda Highton-Smith-Kennington-Jones said goodbye to her friends on the steps of Winchesterfield Manor.

'Please try to be brave, Mrs Smith.' She wrapped her arms around the cook's waist.

'Dear girl.' Mrs Smith sniffled into her tissue, then fished around in her apron pocket to retrieve a small parcel wrapped in greaseproof paper. 'Some brownies for the drive.'

'Oh Mrs Smith, my favourites! You really are the

best brownie cook in the whole world. I'll share them with Mummy and Jacinta. You know, I was thinking you should make them for Kennington's. I'm sure we'd sell kazillions. Imagine: "Mrs Smith's Scrumptious Melt-in-Your-Mouth Chocolate Brownies".' Alice-Miranda underlined the invisible words in the air. 'Wouldn't that be amazing – you'd be famous!'

Mrs Smith turned the colour of beetroot. 'Off you go,' she smiled. 'And please tell Mrs Oliver I'm looking forward to seeing her later in the week.'

Alice-Miranda stepped back and moved along the line.

'Now, you look after those flowers while I'm gone, Mr Charles,' she said, smiling up at her weathered friend. His eyes, the colour of cornflowers, sparkled in the morning sunlight and he brushed a work-worn hand across the corner of his face.

'Ah lass, I'll have those blooms perfect by the time you get back,' he nodded.

Alice-Miranda stepped closer, wrapping her arms around his middle.

'Off with you now,' he said and patted her shoulder.

Mr Plumpton and Miss Reedy stood side by side. His nose glowed red, while she maintained her usual dignified stance.

'Thank you, Miss Reedy.' Alice-Miranda offered her tiny hand, which the English teacher shook most vigorously. 'I've had a wonderful term.'

'You have a lovely break, Alice-Miranda. It's hard to believe you've been here only three months.' Livinia Reedy looked down at her youngest student. The girl was a constant source of amazement.

'And Mr Plumpton, your science lessons have been truly fantastic. I will never in my life forget that volcano experiment. All that frothing and fizzing and then – boom!' Alice-Miranda laughed.

Mr Plumpton's forehead wrinkled. 'That wasn't my best work, Alice-Miranda. Not quite the outcome I was expecting.'

'But Mr Plumpton, it was magnificent – even if it did make a lasting impression on the ceiling and spew that icky liquid all over the lab.'

'Yes, well, I can only imagine how the volcano's vent ended up with a cork wedged in it.' He tried not to, but couldn't help showing an embarrassed smirk.

Next in line stood Mrs Derby. Alice-Miranda

was only just getting used to Miss Higgins's new name.

'You have a lovely holiday, sweetheart,' the young woman beamed.

'Thank you, Miss Higgins, I mean, Mrs Derby,' Alice-Miranda corrected herself.

Mrs Derby knelt down and brushed a stray curl behind Alice-Miranda's ear. The child leaned forward and threw her arms around Mrs Derby's neck.

'Now what was that for?' she asked, as surprised as she had been the first time Alice-Miranda offered such affection.

'Just because,' the tiny girl whispered.

At the end of the line loomed the headmistress, Miss Ophelia Grimm, in a striking magenta suit. Her hair, now swept up loosely, no longer pinned her face into a scowl. Today she was elegant and quite beautiful.

'Alice-Miranda,' she barked sternly, and then as if remembering she was no longer *that* person, she cleared her throat and began again.

'Alice-Miranda.' This time her tone was soft. 'Thank you for your hard work this term. It has been a pleasure.' Her dark eyes smiled and her mouth curved upwards.

'No, thank *you*, Miss Grimm. Winchesterfield-Downsfordvale Academy for Proper Young Ladies really is the most beautiful school in the whole wide world and you are the best headmistress in the world too. Even when you were, well, upset and angry, pretty much all of the time, I knew that wasn't really you. You were far too stylish and lovely to be as mean as all that.' Alice-Miranda stopped suddenly.

Miss Grimm's eyes narrowed.

'What I meant to say, Miss Grimm, is that I knew it wasn't the real you; the one who spied on us and never came out to see the girls and the staff and wouldn't let Mrs Smith take holidays or Mr Charles plant flowers, or Jacinta go to the gymnastics championships—'

'Stop!' Miss Grimm held up her hand.

'But Miss Grimm, what I really meant to say—'

'Enough,' Miss Grimm cut her off again, her steely eyes threatening. 'No more. Do not say another word, Alice-Miranda.'

Suddenly Ophelia's face crumpled and she found herself smiling at this infernal child with her cascading chocolate curls. She bent down to meet Alice-Miranda's brown-eyed gaze.

'Now, Miss Highton-Smith-Kennington-Jones, as your headmistress I am commanding that during this term break you will under no circumstances spend time studying for ridiculous academic tests, nor will you set off on any wilderness walks on your own and you most *definitely* will not train for onerous physical challenges. After what I put you through at the beginning of the term, I expect nothing less than a fortnight of purely childish pursuits befitting that of a girl aged seven and one-quarter.'

'Oh dear, I am sorry, Miss Grimm, but I can't guarantee any of those things,' Alice-Miranda whispered.

'And why ever not, young lady?' Miss Grimm snapped.

'Because, Miss Grimm, I'm actually now seven and a half,' Alice-Miranda beamed.

Before she knew what she was doing, Ophelia Grimm leaned forward and hugged Alice-Miranda tightly.

'Thank you, Miss Grimm.' Alice-Miranda hugged her right back. 'And you and Mr Grump enjoy your honeymoon, too. Goodness knows you've waited long enough for it.'

Now it was Ophelia's turn to blush.

Alice-Miranda ran towards her mother's shiny car parked at the bottom of the steps.

'Come on, darling, time to go home,' Cecelia Highton-Smith called, dabbing a tissue to her eyes.

'Hurry up, Alice-Miranda,' griped Jacinta from the back seat. Then she leant forward and waved furiously out the window. 'Bye everyone!'

The staff could hardly believe just how much things had changed in the eleven and a half weeks Alice-Miranda had been at Winchesterfield-Downsfordvale. And who would have thought that Jacinta Headlington-Bear – the school's former second best tantrum thrower – would ever be invited home for term break?

Chapter 2

'So, Mummy, you survived my first term.' Alice-Miranda turned to her mother sitting beside her in the front seat.

'Yes, I suppose I did,' sniffled Cecelia Highton-Smith as she turned the key in the ignition. The car lurched forward and they were on their way.

'I'm so glad you finally stopped crying.' There was a stern tinge to Alice-Miranda's voice. 'I mean, you have stopped crying, haven't you, Mummy?'

'I'm sorry, darling. It's just that your father and

I missed you so much. It wasn't the same without you romping around the house.'

'Of course it wasn't,' Alice-Miranda replied. 'But you were terribly busy. Daddy told me you were both off all over the place every other day, taking care of the business. So it was much better that you didn't have to worry about me at all. And besides, I saw you and Daddy three times during the term anyway. I can't imagine you had a minute to miss me.'

Alice-Miranda's parents had been caught off guard when their only daughter decided to start boarding school early. Although they expected her to go at some stage, it had come as a quite a shock when she telephoned the school and organized to commence at the beginning of the new school year. But they knew that once she had made up her mind there was no point trying to stop her. And if truth be known, Alice-Miranda was quite right about her parents being busy. Her mother, Cecelia Highton-Smith, had recently become Chairman of the Board of her late father's retail empire. Highton's, the most stylish department stores in the world, sold ladieswear and lingerie, labradors and llamas and everything in between. When Cecelia married Hugh Kennington-Jones, newspapers had heralded their match as the most magnificent retailing merger the world had ever known. With Hugh at the helm of Kennington's, the largest supermarket chain in history, busy was something of an understatement.

'Do you really love it at school?' asked Cecelia as she glanced at her little daughter.

'Oh Mummy, it was everything I could have hoped for and so much more.' Alice-Miranda was practically bursting with enthusiasm as she spoke. 'Wasn't Miss Grimm's wedding the most beautiful ever? Well, except for Miss Higgins's. I suppose they were equally lovely in their own way. Who would have thought I would be a flower girl twice in one term, especially when I didn't even know either of the brides until just a little while ago. And then Jacinta won the championships, which of course she would because she's the best gymnast ever, and Mr Charles won the garden competition – you should have seen his face Mummy, he didn't stop smiling for a week. And our lessons were so wonderful. I hadn't realized my brain could take in so many things all at once. Then we had our swimming carnival – I didn't do very well but I did try, and Millie won seven ribbons. She's incredible! I think she could go to the Olympics. She's pretty amazing at tennis too – maybe she will win Wimbledon as well. Oh, I wish she was coming home with us too . . .'

'Darling, please take a breath,' her mother laughed.

'Ahh,' Alice-Miranda sighed. 'I suppose I do have a fortnight to tell you everything.'

'A fortnight, only a fortnight! Darling, please don't remind me.' Moisture glistened in the corner of her mother's eye. 'I don't know how I'll be able to take you back again in just—'

Alice-Miranda cut her off. 'Mummy, please don't start. We have two whole weeks so let's just enjoy them.' She passed her mother a clean tissue. 'Promise?' she asked, raising her eyebrows.

'All right, but only if I have to,' her mother reluctantly agreed.

'Yes, you have to. Otherwise I'll phone Miss Grimm right this minute and ask if I can stay at school for the holidays,' Alice-Miranda teased, her brown eyes sparkling. 'I'm sure Mr Charles would love some company and Mrs Derby would look after me.'

Her mother immediately changed the subject. 'What about you, Jacinta? Have you had a good term?' Cecelia glanced at her in the rear-vision mirror.

'Yes, Mrs Highton-Smith.'

'Please call me Cecelia, or Cee. Mrs Highton-Smith sounds like my mother.'

'Sorry, Cecelia,' said Jacinta, smiling to herself. 'It *has* been a good term, although it started very badly. I'd been so sick and I was cross with everyone but then Alice-Miranda came, and in the end it really was the best term ever. Who would have thought that she would be able to bring Miss Grimm out of her study after all those years? School is like a different place altogether now. I just wish my parents had been able to get back for the gymnastics championships, but as usual Mummy was tied up somewhere with her friends and Daddy was away on business.'

'Never mind, darling. I'm sure they are very proud of you.' Cecelia fixed her stare on the road ahead.

The silver Range Rover sped along the country lanes, through the village of Winchesterfield and then on to the tiny hamlet of Downsfordvale with its quaint row of whitewashed cottages. The countryside tumbled past and the girls chattered about the term and what they were planning to do at home.

Alice-Miranda swivelled around to look at Jacinta in the back seat. 'I can't wait for you to meet

Bonaparte.' She turned back to her mother. 'Did Max bring him in last week, Mummy?'

'Yes, darling. Max has been very busy working Bony. I think he's been lunging him every day – he told me that he feared the saddle girth would need to be let out a few notches.'

'I don't think Daddy will be able to call him Bony Pony any more by the sounds of that,' Alice-Miranda giggled.

'I hate horses,' Jacinta declared.

'Really? Why? I can't imagine it,' Alice-Miranda replied. 'Bonaparte is a big softie. He wouldn't hurt anyone – and you don't have to ride if you don't want to. There are lots of other things we can do.'

'Well, I won't be going near any horses, that's for sure,' Jacinta stated.

Cecelia glanced in the rear-vision mirror. 'I'm not very good with horses either, Jacinta.'

'It's not that.' Jacinta frowned. 'I'm actually an excellent rider. It's just that I don't like them. They smell.'

Cecelia suppressed a giggle. 'So, what about you and I do something together when Alice-Miranda heads out riding with her father? We could go swimming or perhaps you'd like to do some cooking

15

or read a book? We could even take some rods down to the river and try to catch some of those trout Mr Greening tells me have grown rather large.'

'I'm fantastic at fishing. But I won't be able to touch them at all. I'm allergic,' Jacinta announced.

Cecelia laughed. 'Well, I can't guarantee we'll catch anything but I'm sure we can have some fun trying.' She made a right turn into a sun-dappled lane hemmed on both sides by rough-hewn stone walls. 'Nearly home, girls.'

As the car continued along the lane, Alice-Miranda's attention was diverted by a face peering over the wall. It belonged to a dark-haired boy. He was staring at the road, and as the car went past his tongue shot out at her like a lizard.

'Mummy, did you see that?' Alice-Miranda asked.

'See what?' her mother replied.

'Just back there, a boy looking over the wall. He stuck out his tongue when we drove past,' Alice-Miranda explained.

'Really?' Cecelia glanced at her daughter. 'I wonder who that would be.'

'I've never seen him before,' Alice-Miranda continued.

'How rude!' Jacinta exclaimed.

Alice-Miranda shrugged. 'Perhaps we might find him later when we go for a walk.'

Jacinta scowled. 'I hope not.'

The chimneypots of Highton Hall stood tall in the distance behind a thick stand of poplar trees. The car crunched over the loose gravel and halted at a T-junction.

'Which way?' Cecelia asked.

'Well, I can't wait to see absolutely everyone, but it's getting late and knowing Mrs Oliver, she's quite likely made something extra special for our lunch, so perhaps we should go straight home and then Jacinta and I can go for a walk this afternoon.'

'That's a very good decision. Dolly has been fussing for days and I know she's dying to see you both.'

Dolly Oliver had been the Highton-Smiths's cook for more years than anyone could remember. Alice-Miranda adored her and Mrs Oliver felt the same way about Alice-Miranda.

The two girls nodded in firm agreement and with that Cecelia turned the car left through an imposing set of iron gates into the grounds of Highton Hall.

'Oh, that's a funny little house!' Jacinta exclaimed, craning her neck to get a better look at the gatehouse with its myriad turrets and chimneys. 'Does anyone live there?'

'Yes, do you remember Mr Greening?' Alice-Miranda asked. 'He came to school to help Mr Charles with the flowers.'

'The old man with the grey beard – was that him?' Jacinta replied.

'Yes, that's right. He and Mrs Greening live there.'

'Mr Greening was born in that house,' Cecelia added. 'His father before him was the head gardener here, so they're very much part of the family. They raised four sons who've all grown up and moved away. Now it's just the two of them – and our girl here, when she's at home. I always know where to find Alice-Miranda, especially around four o'clock.'

'Why four o'clock?' Jacinta puzzled.

'Well,' said Alice-Miranda. 'Mrs Greening makes the most delicious cake. It tastes like clouds and has cream frosting that fizzes on your tongue – doesn't it, Mummy? It doesn't have a proper name so I call it Heaven Cake. I've asked Mrs Greening loads of times to share the recipe but she says it's a closely guarded family secret and she'll only give it to me on my twenty-first birthday. I smuggled a piece home once and asked Mrs Oliver if she could make one just like it, but she says there's an ingredient she can't work out – and you know Mrs Oliver is the most wonderful cook in the whole world and a pretty amazing scientist too, so it must be something rare.' Alice-Miranda rubbed her tummy. 'Mr Greening has the most adorable labrador. Her name is Betsy and she's very keen on licking ankles for some strange reason.'

'Well that's just gross.' Jacinta wrinkled her nose.

Alice-Miranda smiled at her mother.

Cecelia steered the car through another set of ornate gates. A broad avenue of oaks opened up and they were home.

Chapter 3

'Mummy, look!' Alice-Miranda exclaimed. 'Everyone's here.'

Several smiling faces waved at them from the front porch. Alice-Miranda unclasped her seatbelt and was out the door in a blink.

'Welcome home, my darling girl,' cried Mrs Oliver. She enveloped Alice-Miranda in her arms. As always she looked neat as a pin – her trademark brown curls set perfectly in place.

'I've missed you so much,' Alice-Miranda

beamed. 'Mrs Smith said to say hello and she's looking forward to seeing you next week.'

Dolly Oliver and Doreen Smith had forged a remarkable friendship during their time cooking together at Winchesterfield-Downsfordvale. Over bubbling pots and sizzling hotplates, they barely drew a breath as they nattered together and exchanged tips. And by the end of the week, Mrs Oliver had invited Mrs Smith home for the holidays to work on her top-secret inventions in the laboratory that occupied the ancient cellars of Highton Hall. She'd recently perfected FDF – Freeze-Dried Foods – and was working on several new recipes to expand her range.

'Hello, Mr Greening.' Alice-Miranda ran to greet him. 'You should see the flowers at school – they're simply amazing! Mr Charles can't stop smiling and whistling, which I think drives Miss Grimm a little mad. Your garden is beautiful too,' she added, looking around at the sweep of lawn dotted with colourful flowerbeds, antique urns and in the centre, three life-sized topiary horses, known affectionately as Bess, Beetle and Bobbin. The gardens at Highton Hall were his pride and joy.

'Thank you, miss,' he said, smiling at Alice-Miranda. 'It certainly has been quiet around here without you. Mrs Greening is looking forward to a four o'clock visit – if that's all right with your mother.' He winked. Alice-Miranda winked right back and touched her fingertip to the side of her nose.

'Hello, Mrs Shillingsworth!' Alice-Miranda lunged forward to hug the woman standing beside Mrs Oliver. 'It's so lovely to be home. I can't wait to tell you about school and all the wonderful things that have happened, and I want to hear everything that's been going on here too,' she prattled.

Mrs Shillingsworth nodded.

Alice-Miranda looked around. 'Where's Daddy?'

'Sorry, darling,' her mother answered. 'Your father had some urgent business in town this morning but he hopes to be back early this evening.'

'Well,' Alice-Miranda beamed at the trio in front of her, 'I'll just catch up with the rest of my family first.' Suddenly she clasped her hands to her mouth. 'Jacinta!' She raced around to the other side of the car and grabbed Jacinta's hand, tugging her towards the porch. 'Please forgive me for being so rude. May I introduce my family? Everyone, this is my good friend Jacinta Headlington-Bear. You know Mrs Oliver of course.'

Mrs Oliver stepped forward and gave Jacinta a warm hug.

'And then there's Mr Greening, who I think you met when he came to school to help Mr Charles.'

Jacinta smiled and nodded.

'And this is Mrs Shillingsworth. She runs the *whole* house.'

Mrs Shillingsworth blushed a deep shade of crimson. She shook her head at Alice-Miranda and furrowed her brows. 'My dear, I have an army of helpers.'

A tall woman with a sturdy frame, Mrs Shillingsworth was obviously fit for the task. Her grey hair was tamed into an elegant chignon. Her practical navy skirt and crisp white shirt gave her the air of someone who simply got on with it – whatever *it* may be.

'I'm so sorry; I should have introduced you straight away. I must have left my manners back at school,' Alice-Miranda tutted to herself.

'Don't worry,' Jacinta grinned. 'I've been known to leave *my* manners in another country.'

'Well, I don't know about the rest of you, but I could murder a cup of tea,' said Cecelia, as she unloaded the girls' bags from the back of the car.

Mr Greening offered to take them up for her.

'I'll put the pot on,' said Mrs Oliver, and bustled away.

'And I think someone has been rather busy baking some extra special treats in honour of your homecoming,' Mrs Shillingsworth added, nodding her head towards Mrs Oliver's back.

'Come on, then!' Alice-Miranda took Jacinta's hand. 'What are we waiting for?' The group marched inside.

Chapter 4

The scrubbed pine table groaned under the weight of Mrs Oliver's homecoming feast. Chicken sandwiches, miniature roast beef rolls and salmon tarts sat alongside apple teacake, cream buns, chocolate éclairs and Alice-Miranda's favourite devil's food cake.

Alice-Miranda chatted about her teachers.

'You know, Mummy, Miss Reedy is amazing. We have the loveliest chats about books and writers. She adores Mr Dahl as much as I do.'

Jacinta told them about the headmistress, Miss Grimm, and all the changes at the school over the past term.

'And just wait until you see Mrs Smith,' Alice-Miranda went on. 'She looks wonderful and her dinners have been simply scrumptious.'

Mrs Shillingsworth frowned. 'Well in my day, school was different altogether. There were certainly no friendly chats with teachers. Many's a day I spent with a roll of newspaper in my knickers to avoid the sting of the paddle and as for the food, my goodness, I think you lot must be spoiled silly. I clearly remember buckets of thick brown porridge and sloppy mash floating in a sea of watery vegetables. I think we only ever had meat once a year for Christmas.'

Alice-Miranda giggled. 'I hope they didn't give you porridge and mash together. That would be truly disgusting.'

'Oh Shilly, you do paint a terrible picture,' Cecelia laughed. 'Fortunately things have come rather a long way in the past few years.'

'Few years,' Mrs Oliver snorted. 'I think there's more than a few years since our Shilly here was at school.'

'Well, it didn't do me any harm,' Shilly said with a scowl. 'Toughening up, that's what children these days need. Soft, I say, the lot of them.'

Jacinta shifted uncomfortably in her seat. She wasn't at all sure about Mrs Shillingsworth. Her eyebrows had a terrible habit of knitting together even when she seemed to be smiling.

But Alice-Miranda simply grinned at the house-keeper. 'That was the best lunch ever.' She folded her napkin in front of her, skipped around to Mrs Oliver and wrapped her arms around her neck.

'Steady there, young lady.' Mrs Oliver's teacup wobbled and she placed it with a sharp chink back onto the saucer. 'Now, to what do I owe such grand affection?'

'Just because,' Alice-Miranda said and pecked Mrs Oliver's powdered cheek.

'Darling, why don't you take Jacinta upstairs,' her mother suggested. She turned to Jacinta. 'You can decide if you'd like to share Alice-Miranda's bedroom or have a room of your own.'

'Thank you, Mrs Hight– I mean, Cecelia,' said Jacinta. She and Alice-Miranda excused themselves, and Alice-Miranda led the way up the kitchen staircase.

Jacinta was wide-eyed as she took in her new surroundings. 'It's an enormous house,' she said, bounding after her guide. 'Have you always lived here?'

'Well, it's been in Mummy's family for ever – I think about two hundred years. So I've always lived here and Mummy, Granny and Pa before that and I suppose quite a few of the great grannies and pas as well,' Alice-Miranda replied.

A grand Georgian mansion set over four levels, including a labyrinth of cellars, Highton Hall sat atop a rise in the middle of a vast 6000 hectare estate. It was widely regarded as one of the most beautiful homes in the country. It boasted an east and west library, long gallery and ballroom among its fifty-odd rooms; guests often became lost in its grandeur.

'Do you know, I'm sure there are rooms I've never even been into?' Alice-Miranda continued. 'Last year I stumbled on a whole suite I can't remember seeing before. Sometimes I think this house is a TARDIS.'

'It's a bit like school really, although with much better curtains,' said Jacinta. 'There are places I've only just discovered there too. Did you know that there's a secret passage off the science room?'

'Really?' Alice-Miranda gasped. 'Where does it go?'

'I don't know,' Jacinta replied. 'Ashima told me about it. She said she overheard Alethea bragging that she had found it and no one was allowed to go there except if she said so.'

Alethea Goldsworthy had been Head Prefect at Winchesterfield-Downsfordvale for the first couple of weeks of term – until to her horror of horrors Miss Grimm discovered that she was an awful bully, a cheat and a liar. She had left the school in rather a rush, after she was caught cheating in a sailing race against Alice-Miranda.

'Well, Alethea's not there any more so next term we'll have to go exploring.' Alice-Miranda's brown eyes twinkled.

The girls climbed the long flight of stairs and arrived in a very grand hallway, at least five metres wide. A plush Chinese carpet in hues of pink, green and blue ran its full length with various chairs and side tables lining the passage. Huge portraits in heavily gilded frames adorned the pale-mint papered walls.

'Are those your relatives?' Jacinta asked, pointing towards the paintings. She could have sworn she saw one of the figures turn its head as she passed.

'Yes, but don't worry – we haven't had any problems with them lately,' Alice-Miranda replied.

Jacinta gulped. She studied one particularly large picture of a young woman wearing a soft buttercup-coloured gown and a diamond tiara. She looked vaguely familiar.

'My room's this way,' said Alice-Miranda. She grabbed Jacinta's hand and led her to the very end of the corridor. She turned the ancient ceramic handle and pushed open the oak door to reveal one of the prettiest rooms Jacinta had ever seen. In the middle stood a large four-poster bed dressed in the most delicate of pale pink floral bedclothes. In one corner was an enormous doll's house complete with felt grass lawn and in another a gleaming white rocking horse. A large Persian carpet took up most of the room and luxurious cream curtains tumbled to the floor, tied back with fist-sized silver tassels. A pair of cedar armoires stood guard either side of a black marble fireplace in the middle of one wall. Directly opposite, two doors led to who knows where.

Jacinta inspected the doll's house. 'This is lovely,' she sighed, being careful not to touch anything.

'Can you see what it is?' Alice-Miranda asked.

'It's very big. And so perfect. Look at the detail on those windows.' Jacinta leaned down to look inside. 'There's a doll's house in there!' she exclaimed, peering into one of the front windows on the second floor. She shielded her eyes to get a better look. 'And a rocking horse, just like yours,' she stood back. 'It's *your* house!' Jacinta beamed.

'Mr Greening's father made it for Mummy when she was a little girl. I think it's the most perfect doll's house ever.' Alice-Miranda lifted part of the roof to reveal an attic room. 'Mummy says it took him two years to build it. He used an old set of plans and Granny helped him with all the details. It's exactly the same as the Hall, just in miniature. In fact, I suppose if I study the doll's house I might find some more of those mysterious rooms I've not see before,' she added as an afterthought.

'Are you allowed to play with it?' Jacinta stepped back as Alice-Miranda pulled a trunk from the attic.

'Of course,' she said. 'Mummy and Aunt Charlotte played with it all the time when they were little and it's always been here.'

Jacinta frowned. 'Well, that's sensible.'

'What do you mean?' Alice-Miranda asked.

31

'I have a doll's house too, but I'm not allowed to touch it because it once belonged to a princess and Mummy says it won't be valuable any more if I play with it. I told her that wasn't fair but she decided it would be best if I just looked at it – so now it's locked away inside a glass case.' Jacinta rolled her eyes.

'But that's silly,' said Alice-Miranda with a shake of her head. 'Of course you should play with it. I'll talk to your mother. Maybe she just doesn't understand about doll's houses.' Alice-Miranda picked up a doll dressed in a navy skirt and white shirt. She looked a bit like Mrs Shillingsworth.

'I don't know,' Jacinta replied. 'But I'm sure you won't change her mind.'

'Well you can play with this house all day long if you'd like,' Alice-Miranda said decisively and handed Jacinta the doll.

Chapter 5

After a tour of the bedrooms on the second floor, Jacinta decided that she would like to sleep in the room beside Alice-Miranda's which shared an adjoining bathroom.

'I hope you don't mind,' said Jacinta. She flopped open the lid of her suitcase. 'I'm sure you'll be happy to be back in your own room and honestly, I'm quite fine on my own too. After school, where there's always someone in the same room, it's a bit of a novelty really.'

'Of course I don't mind at all.' Alice-Miranda began unpacking Jacinta's clothes into the tallboy opposite the bed.

The room was generously proportioned and had a large carpeted area where Jacinta thought she might do some stretching and floor work. She was aiming to go to the junior world championships and couldn't afford to stop training, even though it was holidays.

'Besides,' said Alice-Miranda, 'this room has lots of space and I thought you might want to do some stretching. It might be a bit small for tumbling but the Great Hall downstairs would be perfect for that.'

'Can you read minds?' Jacinta asked.

Alice-Miranda grinned.

After they finished unpacking, Alice-Miranda suggested they go and explore the estate.

'I've got loads of people I want you to meet – and we do have that special invitation from Mrs Greening at four o'clock. And I've been thinking about that boy in the laneway,' Alice-Miranda pondered out loud. 'I wonder who he is.'

'Well, whoever he is, someone needs to teach him some manners,' Jacinta replied.

'I think I'll go and put on my old jeans in case we find some good trees to climb. You should get changed too.' Alice-Miranda walked to the bathroom door and headed through into her own room.

Five minutes later the girls met in the hallway. Jacinta had changed from her school dress into navy pants and a short-sleeved striped navy top. Alice-Miranda wore a faded pair of denim jeans with a pink shirt. Both girls had trainers on their feet.

'Now I feel like I'm home,' said Alice-Miranda, brushing minuscule creases from her shirt. 'Come on.'

She ran down the hallway to the central staircase, where she promptly leaped onto the banister rail. Jacinta followed at her heels.

'Alice-Miranda,' Jacinta whispered urgently. 'Mrs Shillingsworth is coming.'

'Good, she can time me.'

'Alice-Miranda,' Mrs Shillingsworth barked. 'You wait right there, young lady.'

The girls turned their heads in unison to catch sight of Mrs Shillingsworth, a stack of fresh towels in her arms, charging towards them.

'Get down,' Jacinta urged.

'It's OK. Really it is,' Alice-Miranda assured her friend.

Mrs Shillingsworth set her fluffy tower down on a Louis chair opposite the top of the staircase. She fished around in her skirt pocket and retrieved what looked to be a rather large stopwatch.

'I thought you were going to have a practice run without me. I believe that just before you took yourself off to that school of yours, you had managed a new record.' Mrs Shillingsworth fumbled in the other pocket and pulled out a neatly folded piece of paper. From behind her ear she produced a small pencil. 'Ahh, here it is, eleven seconds from the top to the bottom.'

'I'm a bit out of practice, Shilly; I don't know if it will be a record breaker. Count me down.' Alice-Miranda gripped tight and wiggled her bottom.

'Three, two, one!'

The tiny child giggled as she whizzed down the gigantic spiral staircase, landing with a delicate jump at the bottom.

'Stop!' she shouted back up to Mrs Shillingsworth, who was leaning over the balcony next to Jacinta.

'I can't believe you just did that,' said Jacinta, shaking her head.

'What was the time, Shilly?' Alice-Miranda shouted.

'That would be twelve seconds,' she replied. 'But I do think your record was set the day after Daisy polished the staircase. And what about you, Miss Jacinta? Are you eager to throw yourself down the Highton Hall rollercoaster?'

'Well, it does look fun.' Jacinta eyed the banister. 'And I suppose in the absence of a beam or bars to train on, this is the next best thing.'

'Go on,' Alice-Miranda urged. 'Hop up and give it a go. Just loosen your grip and enjoy the ride.'

Jacinta climbed nimbly to the top and positioned herself as Alice-Miranda had done before her.

Mrs Shillingsworth reset her watch. 'On your mark, get set, GO!'

Jacinta squealed as she whizzed down the rail. Her dismount was quite stunning and she finished with a flourish, as though she'd just completed a double somersault from the beam. Alice-Miranda clapped enthusiastically and was joined by her mother who had entered the hallway in time to see Jacinta zoom past.

Cecelia clapped loudly. 'That was magnificent.'

'It was brilliant,' Jacinta laughed.

'What was Jacinta's time?' Cecelia called up to Mrs Shillingsworth.

'Well, she's a speedy one, ma'am. Eleven point four seconds. If you don't look out, Alice-Miranda, I think you might lose your crown,' she frowned.

'I don't mind.' Alice-Miranda hugged her friend. 'Mummy, we're going for a walk. I want Jacinta to meet everyone and then we might pop over to see Mrs Greening.'

Cecelia put her hands on her hips. 'Mmm, I thought you might want to do that. Just mind you leave enough room for Dolly's roast,' she said with a smile.

Alice-Miranda kissed her mother on the cheek, grabbed Jacinta by the hand and the two girls hurtled off into the garden.

'I can't believe I just did that,' Jacinta said as she bounded along beside her friend. 'I mean, I know we sometimes try to do it in the boarding house but that rail's a bit splintery and it hurts like mad unless you've got thick pants on. My mother would have a fit if she saw me riding your banister rail.'

Alice-Miranda grinned. 'I think it was made to be ridden. Mummy and Daddy sometimes join in and Shilly times us all. Once we even coaxed Mrs Oliver into having a turn. She's very proud of her record – for the slowest ride ever. It's a bit of a family tradition.'

Jacinta stopped and stared at the ground. 'I don't think we have any family traditions.'

'Well we have tons – and you're most welcome to join in with them anytime you like.' Alice-Miranda pulled her friend in the direction of the field.

Chapter 6

Alice-Miranda turned the handle of the weathered timber door in the middle of the high stone wall that stretched the length of the garden. The two girls entered the long meadow. It was dotted with vast oaks, all just begging to be climbed.

'Where are we going?' Jacinta asked.

Alice-Miranda pointed towards a row of poplars. 'Over there.'

Beyond them Jacinta could just make out the top of a roof and some chimneypots. 'I want you to meet my friends Jasper and Poppy. Jasper is nine and he's loads of fun and Poppy is the sweetest five-year-old you'll ever meet. Their father Heinrich looks after the farm and sometimes their mother Lily helps Mummy in the house – when we have parties and things. Then we'll go and see Daisy and Granny Bert too.'

The girls were walking under the branches of a very large oak tree when suddenly something rustled in the leaves above.

'Ow,' Jacinta complained. She rubbed her head and looked around for the offending missile.

'What was it?' Alice-Miranda scanned the ground and found a little stone. She bent down and picked it up. 'I thought oak trees produced acorns, not pebbles.'

The girls peered into the plush canopy but couldn't see any delinquent creatures.

'Ow!' Alice-Miranda squeaked as a larger pebble glanced off the top of her head and hit the ground with a light thud. 'Whoever or whatever you are, please stop throwing stones. It's really not very nice,' she called into the tree.

A sliver of light shone through the emerald limbs and suddenly another pebble hit Jacinta.

'Right, that's it,' Jacinta swung into action. 'I'm coming up there so whatever you are, you'd better watch out.'

Jacinta scaled the low branches quickly, swinging her legs up onto the higher boughs. As her friend climbed, Alice-Miranda was distracted by a flash of blue. It seemed that the hidden rogue was trying to make a getaway. A figure landed on the ground right in front of her.

'Stop right there,' Alice-Miranda commanded. 'Please,' she added.

It was the boy from the lane. Before he had time to make an escape, Alice-Miranda held out her hand and said, 'Hello, my name is Alice-Miranda Highton-Smith-Kennington-Jones and I am very pleased to meet you.'

They boy stared at Alice-Miranda as if he was observing an alien species.

'I know who you are,' he spat.

'Well, please don't think me rude,' Alice-Miranda continued, 'but I don't recall us meeting before now, although I'm sure that I saw you in the laneway a little while ago.'

'We haven't met before,' the boy replied.

Jacinta jumped to the ground beside her friend.

'That wasn't very nice you know, throwing stones at us.' Jacinta glared fiercely.

'Well I'm not particularly nice,' he said, his eyes narrowing. 'In fact, I'm not nice at all.'

'Who told you that?' Alice-Miranda asked.

'Everyone,' the boy replied.

'Well that's just silly. You don't know everyone do you? Not everyone in the whole world. That would be impossible. I mean, my daddy knows quite a lot of people but he would say that it's just a tiny number really out of the whole wide world—'

'Do you ever shut up?' the boy interrupted.

Alice-Miranda smiled at him. 'I'm sorry. You haven't even had a moment to tell us your name.'

'Why would I tell you my name?' he sneered.

Alice-Miranda nodded at her friend. 'Well, this is Jacinta Headlington-Bear – she goes to Winchesterfield-Downsfordvale Academy for Proper Young Ladies with me and she has come home to spend the holidays.' She tried again. 'And you are?'

'You don't need to know,' he said bluntly.

'But it would be so much better if we knew your name. Then we could be friends,' Alice-Miranda insisted.

'Friends? With you?' the boy snorted. 'You've got to be joking.'

'Why? I would never joke about being friends . . .' Alice-Miranda began.

Without warning, the boy reached out and shoved Alice-Miranda so hard that she fell backwards to the ground. She landed with a thump on her bottom. While Jacinta was helping her back to her feet the boy turned and ran towards the stand of poplars, disappearing through the hedge.

'Hey!' Jacinta called. 'What did you do that for?'

Alice-Miranda dusted herself off.

'That was interesting,' she frowned.

'Interesting! I think he's the most horrid boy I've ever seen.' Jacinta's cheeks were an angry red. 'Let's go after him. Someone needs to teach that little monster a lesson,' she added.

'Don't worry – he won't get far. He must be here visiting someone. The village is quite a long walk away so I can't imagine he's come all the way from there. Let's go and find Jasper and Poppy – they might know who he is. Perhaps he just needs some friends.'

'He doesn't deserve friends,' Jacinta huffed. 'And he definitely didn't want to be friends with you.'

The two girls continued on their journey. They ducked through the hedge and came out near an ancient stone farmhouse. It was beautifully preserved and had a lovely garden trimmed with hollyhocks.

Alice-Miranda led Jacinta down the side of the house and through to the backyard. A tall blond woman was hanging sheets on a clothesline.

'Lily!' Alice-Miranda called. The woman snipped the last peg onto a white sheet and turned around to greet them.

'Hello there, young lady. It's wonderful to see you,' she said, giving Alice-Miranda a hug. 'And who's this you've brought with you?' Lily's tanned face beamed.

'Lily, this is my friend, Jacinta Headlington-Bear. We go to school together and she's going to spend the holidays here with us.'

'Pleased to make your acquaintance, Jacinta,' Lily smiled. 'I know two children who have been dying for you to get home, Alice-Miranda.' Lily picked up her empty basket and the girls followed her to the back door.

'You didn't see a boy come through here a few minutes ago, did you?' Jacinta asked. 'Dark hair – a little bit taller than me?'

Lily hesitated. 'Why?'

'Well,' Jacinta began, 'he was in one of the oak trees in the field and the little brat was throwing stones at us and then he pushed Alice-Miranda to the ground and ran off. Someone needs to give him a good talking to.'

'Oh dear.' Lily fiddled with her hair. 'I'm afraid I do know who that boy is.'

'He seemed to know me but I can't say I remember ever seeing him before,' said Alice-Miranda, puzzled.

'You're right – you wouldn't have seen him before. I imagine he knows who you are from seeing some of the photographs of you with Jasper and Poppy.'

Jacinta was indignant. 'Well he needs to learn some manners.'

'Come in, girls. Jasper is upstairs in his room and Poppy is colouring in the kitchen. They'll be thrilled to see you,' said Lily, avoiding any further discussion of her nephew.

Chapter 7

Poppy squealed with delight the moment Alice-Miranda entered the kitchen. She squeezed her tightly and immediately invited both girls to sit down and colour in. Lily called Jasper to come down from his room four times before he finally emerged, dragging his feet.

'Muuum, I was in the middle of a battle,' he protested. Then he caught sight of Alice-Miranda.

'You're back!' Jasper exclaimed as he rushed to give Alice-Miranda an enthusiastic hug. Spying

Jacinta at the table beside his sister, he quickly let go and turned a very bright shade of pink.

'You didn't tell me we had guests,' he whispered to Lily, who was getting some drinks organized.

'You didn't ask,' she replied. 'And Alice-Miranda is hardly a guest, darling.'

'You know what I mean, Mum.'

Alice-Miranda introduced her friend. 'This is Jacinta Headlington-Bear. She's staying with us for the holidays.'

'Hello.' Jasper looked up shyly. 'It's nice to meet you.'

Jacinta hadn't met many boys but Jasper seemed the politest one she had ever encountered. He was certainly the opposite of that other horrid boy. Jasper was sweet and friendly and there was something about his smile that made her want to smile right back.

After sampling some delicious homemade lemonade the children went upstairs to play. Poppy tagged along despite her brother's protests. In a small room under the eaves, Jasper showed Alice-Miranda and Jacinta an old trestle table on which he had recreated a battlefield resplendent with trenches, trees, tanks and various other artillery installations. He was explaining how he had recently added a village when Jacinta piped up.

'We met an awful boy before – in the field,' she began.

'Oh,' Jasper replied absently.

'He was hiding in one of the oak trees and pelting stones at us. He hit me twice and he hit Alice-Miranda once too.' Jacinta folded her arms in front of her. 'Your mother said that she knew him.'

'Where does he come from, Jasper?' Alice-Miranda asked gently.

'He belongs to us,' Poppy replied. 'His mummy doesn't want him any more. And he doesn't have a daddy.'

'That's not true. Aunty Kitty's just gone away for a while.' Jasper glared at his chatterbox sister and then continued playing with his tiny tin men, lining them up row by row.

'He got spelled.' Poppy poked her tongue out at her brother.

'Spelled? Do you mean *expelled*, from school? Is that true?' asked Alice-Miranda as she inspected one of the soldiers.

'He's a bad boy.' Poppy nodded her head.

'I don't want to talk about him. Stop telling tales, Poppy. You know what Mum said.'

Alice-Miranda smiled at Poppy.

Before she had time to say anything else Jasper stood up. 'Let's go and see Daisy and Granny Bert.' He placed a soldier back on the table. 'She's been ill, you know.'

'Who?' Alice-Miranda asked.

'Who what?' Jasper replied.

'Who's been sick? Daisy or Granny Bert?'

Jasper looked puzzled.

'Granny Bert, of course. Don't you listen?' He rolled his eyes.

The children traipsed downstairs and Jasper informed his mother of their plans.

'Would you mind taking this with you? Daisy and Granny might like some treats.' Lily handed Alice-Miranda a wicker basket containing a rectangular lemon cake with passionfruit frosting, a jar of homemade cherry jam and two fat pears.

Alice-Miranda inhaled deeply. 'That cake smells delicious. But I promise we won't touch it. Jacinta and I have been invited for afternoon tea with Mrs Greening – and I'm hoping she's made Heaven Cake.'

'Thanks, sweetheart. Now don't stay too long. It doesn't take much for Granny Bert to get tired.' Lily turned her attention to Jasper and Poppy. 'And you two come straight back afterwards, please. I think there must have been a tornado in a couple of bedrooms upstairs.' She raised her eyebrows.

Jasper frowned and Poppy wrinkled her nose.

The group set off through the front garden, out the gate and down the lane. They passed the main sheds where Jasper and Poppy's father was tinkering with one of the tractors.

'Hello, Daddy.' Poppy waved. Her father looked up and waved back. 'Hello zere, you lot. Alice-Miranda, it's good to have you home again,' Heinrich said in his thick German accent.

'It's lovely to be home, Heinrich. We're off to visit Daisy and Granny Bert. We'll see you later,' she called.

Further along the laneway there was another pretty little house, partially hidden behind a stone wall covered in the most delicate of pink Cécile Brunner roses. The cottage was almost an exact replica of the gatehouse with its turrets and chimneys.

Alice-Miranda handed Jacinta the basket of goodies and went to unlatch the front gate. Just then, the boy who was responsible for the stone throwing appeared from behind the hedge on the opposite side of the lane.

'Hello, Lucas,' Poppy greeted him.

'What do you want – Lucassss?' hissed Jacinta, shooting him a smug stare. 'Have you come to apologise?'

He ignored both girls' words completely and stalked closer.

'What's in the basket?' he demanded as a faint waft of lemon cake escaped from under the tea towel.

'Some treats for Daisy and Granny Bert,' Alice-Miranda replied.

Lucas lifted the towel.

'Hey, what are you doing?' Jacinta pulled the basket away but not quickly enough. He reached in and picked up one of the pears, immediately biting into its green skin.

'Why, you!' Jacinta seethed.

'Lucas, that was for Granny and Daisy.' Alice-Miranda frowned. 'I'm sure if you wanted a pear you could ask Lily for one.'

'Why would I ask her for anything,' he said, still tearing into the juicy fruit. 'So is this your girlfriend,

Jasper? The one in all those pictures with you – from the big house?' he teased.

'Stop it,' Jasper ordered.

'Or what?' Lucas countered.

'Lucas, Jasper is one of my best friends and I do love him of course, but we are both far too young for romance, if that's what you mean,' Alice-Miranda interrupted.

'I do love him of course . . .' Lucas mimicked Alice-Miranda, pouted, and then noisily kissed the back of his hand.

'Leave us alone, Lucas,' Jasper shouted. 'Go home!'

'I'd love to,' Lucas glared at Jasper, his ebony eyes drilling straight through his cousin. Lucas took off through the hedge and disappeared into the field beyond.

Jacinta was fuming, Jasper red-faced but Poppy just smiled.

'Come on. Let's get this cake inside.' Alice-Miranda led the group through the gateway, down the path and around to the side of the cottage.

'Hello, Daisy, Granny, it's Alice-Miranda,' she called cheerily as she opened the door into the kitchen.

A slight young woman with shoulder-length blonde hair was standing at the sink. She looked to be dabbing her eyes with a tissue.

'Daisy, are you all right?' asked Alice-Miranda as she approached her. The woman didn't seem to hear. 'Daisy? Is everything OK?'

She swivelled around, surprised to hear Alice-Miranda's voice.

'Oh,' Daisy let out a little cry. 'It *is* you. I thought I must have been imagining.'

Alice-Miranda ran forward and threw her arms around Daisy's tiny waist.

'It's so lovely to be home,' she said. 'But you look sad.' Alice-Miranda's stomach knotted. 'Is everything all right? Is Granny OK?' Daisy absently stroked the top of Alice-Miranda's head.

'Sorry – I, I've just had a visitor.' She smiled tensely at the children. 'Yes, yes. Granny's getting stronger every day. She had pneumonia but she's well on the mend. Plenty of fluids and rest – Dr Marsh has looked in most days. I think she'll be back on her feet again come the end of the week.'

Alice-Miranda introduced Jacinta, who promptly set the basket on the table. 'I'm afraid there's only one pear – *we* had a visitor too,' Jacinta said, her eyebrows knitting together.

'A visitor?' Daisy looked perplexed.

Alice-Miranda shook her head at Jacinta. She thought Daisy looked as though she had her own worries and there was nothing that could be done about Lucas now anyway.

She changed the subject. 'Nothing to fuss about. I can tell you this cake looks rather good. It's lemon with passionfruit icing.'

'Please thank Lily for me.' Daisy set the contents of the basket out on the table. 'Would you like some? I'm about to put the pot on,' she asked.

'No thanks. We've just had lemonade and next we're off to see Mrs Greening for afternoon tea. I thought we would pop in and see you and Granny and then we'll be off – but I promise we'll be back again soon,' Alice-Miranda said.

Daisy nodded, still looking distracted. 'Oh, OK. Run up and see her then. She should be awake. Tell her I'll bring some tea shortly.'

The children bounded upstairs. If Granny Bert wasn't awake beforehand she certainly would be now.

Chapter 8

A little while later, the two girls said goodbye to Poppy and Jasper outside Rose Cottage. 'You'd better get home,' Alice-Miranda reminded the reluctant pair.

'I'd much rather come with you,' Jasper sighed, before heading off with his little sister in tow.

Granny Bert was certainly on the mend. Propped up on a mountain of pillows, she had spent the whole time huffing and grumbling that her tea was late. Alice-Miranda laughed and said that she couldn't understand what everyone had been so worried about. Clearly Granny Bert was almost as good as new.

She made them promise to come back again tomorrow and take her for a walk around the garden. If she had to have a wheelchair, she said, it might as well be put to good use. Before they left she demanded that Alice-Miranda find her some lipstick. 'I feel naked without my face on,' she had said, flinching at her reflection in the hand mirror she picked up from the cluttered bedside table.

'Goodness, Granny Bert has a lot to say,' Jacinta commented as they headed down the laneway. 'Is she always like that?'

'Oh yes – and usually much worse,' Alice-Miranda laughed. 'But she doesn't often get muddled up with names. I can't imagine why she insisted on calling you Annabelle the whole time.'

'Yes, I mean I could understand if she thought my name was Jasmine, perhaps, or even Jessica but Annabelle was a bit far off the mark,' Jacinta commented. 'Is she really your granny?'

'Oh no, not at all. She's Daisy's granny. But we've always called her Granny Bert – her real name is Albertine. She used to work in the house a long time ago – before Shilly. She ran the whole place when there were loads more staff and house parties every other weekend. Mummy says that she was incredible and everyone loved her.'

'I can't imagine,' Jacinta scoffed.

'She's quite good fun really. Just you wait and see. I can guarantee that once she's completely well, she'll be up to her old tricks again,' Alice-Miranda countered.

The girls skipped on along the laneway towards the gatehouse and Mrs Greening's much anticipated cake. A grand avenue of oaks lined the path and the afternoon sun played tricks with dapples and shadows through the canopy.

They heard in the distance the whine of a powerful engine.

'I wonder who that is.' Alice-Miranda turned and caught sight of a large black sedan speeding away from the back of Rose Cottage. It was creating rather a lot of dust as it accelerated towards them. 'I didn't notice a car when we were at Daisy and Granny's. Did you?' she asked Jacinta.

'No, but Daisy did say something about a visitor, didn't she?' Jacinta replied.

'They must have gone out the back door through

the utility room before we arrived,' Alice-Miranda decided.

'Well, whoever it is seems to be in rather a hurry now.' Jacinta grabbed Alice-Miranda's hand and they jumped back from the road just as the car roared past.

It had dark tinted windows and was travelling at such speed it was impossible to see who was inside.

'Maniac!' Jacinta called after them. 'You'll kill someone!'

Alice-Miranda watched as the vehicle turned left and headed for the main road. She wasn't used to seeing strange cars on the estate – especially not being driven at such pace. She felt a twinge in her tummy and a strange feeling that something wasn't quite right.

The girls walked back onto the road. 'Oh, I see where we are,' Jacinta said as she caught sight of Highton Hall in the distance. 'We've come around in a big loop.'

Her words interrupted Alice-Miranda's thoughts. 'Come on,' Alice-Miranda said, dismissing the strange feelings from her mind. She grabbed Jacinta's hand and started running towards the gatehouse. 'I'm starving.'

Jacinta followed closely behind as Alice-Miranda unlatched the garden gate and bounced down a pathway bordered by delphiniums, hollyhocks and hydrangeas. The warm afternoon air exhaled the most delicious scent. Alice-Miranda ducked through an archway to the side of the path and raced across the velvet lawn towards the back of the house. 'Betsy,' she called. 'Betsy, where are you?'

A gruff bark echoed in reply before Betsy whizzed around the corner to greet the girls.

'Hello, you!' Alice-Miranda threw her arms around the labrador's neck.

Mr Greening appeared. 'Hello, there. You'd better come inside. Mrs Greening has just taken something out of the oven.' He winked at Jacinta.

'Ah, heaven,' Alice-Miranda sighed.

Chapter 9

Mrs Greening bustled around the kitchen pouring cups of sugary white tea which she set down gently in front of the girls. A huge cake with lemon-tinted frosting adorned the centre of the table.

'You can do the honours, dear.' She motioned at the knife in front of Mr Greening. He promptly set about slicing two large wedges of cake, one each for Jacinta and Alice-Miranda. 'Half that size for me please,' Mrs Greening requested, placing a milky cup of tea in front of her husband.

'And twice that size for me, eh?' He winked at Alice-Miranda and Jacinta.

'Goodness, that stomach of yours will never be flat again,' Mrs Greening tutted.

Jacinta finished her first mouthful. 'Alice-Miranda was certainly telling the truth about your cake. It *is* heaven. I wish someone in my family could cook cakes as good as this.'

Mrs Greening blushed. 'That young lady has always been one to write people up. Ever since she was the tiniest wee thing.'

'No I don't,' Alice-Miranda protested. 'I just tell the truth that's all. And the truth is that you make possibly the best cake in the entire world. Although you'd better not tell Mrs Oliver, or Mrs Smith when she comes next week, because they're both pretty excellent cooks too.'

Mr and Mrs Greening exchanged knowing looks and couldn't help but smile.

'So what have you been doing this afternoon?' asked Mrs Greening.

'We saw Granny Bert on the way over,' Alice-Miranda stated. 'I think she must be quite well again.'

'Was she complaining?' Mr Greening smiled.

'She sure was.' Jacinta rolled her eyes. 'And she kept calling me Annabelle.'

'You know, if they had whining as an Olympic sport that woman would win the gold medal every time,' Mr Greening laughed.

'Harold Greening, you behave yourself,' Mrs Greening scolded. 'Granny's just getting old. I think she's starting to forget things, that's all.'

'And we saw Poppy and Jasper and we met a boy called Lucas,' said Alice-Miranda.

'He stole a pear and he threw stones at us in the field and pushed Alice-Miranda over. He's mean,' Jacinta declared.

Mrs Greening bit her lip and frowned.

'Yes, I think Lily's got her hands full at the moment. I've had a couple of run-ins with the lad myself,' Mr Greening added.

'Who is he?' Alice-Miranda asked.

Mrs Greening gave her husband a meaningful look and shook her head.

'Well, you girls had better be off home then,' said Mr Greening. He folded his napkin and placed it on the table.

'Do you know anything about him?' Alice-Miranda tried again.

'He's none of your concern, young lady.'

'But, I'd really like to be his friend,' Alice-Miranda tried again.

'No buts, Alice-Miranda. You can't fix everything and sometimes things just have to work themselves out. Now off you go and don't blame me if you can't eat all your dinner.' Mrs Greening busied herself clearing the teacups and plates into a stack on the sink.

'We won't,' said Alice-Miranda, folding her napkin too.

'Thank you for tea, Mrs Greening.' Jacinta pushed her chair out and carried the cake tray to the sideboard where she placed it down carefully.

'It was my pleasure, dear,' Mrs Greening replied. 'Now you'd better get a move on or the phone will start ringing any moment.'

After much tickling of ankles in the garden (to Jacinta's disgust), the girls finally tore themselves away from Betsy. They headed back towards the Hall with the sun low in the sky and casting shadows over the driveway.

'I can hear Birdy!' Alice-Miranda stopped to listen.

'Do you mean your helicopter? You must have bionic hearing because I can't hear a thing – except that cow over there,' Jacinta replied.

Alice-Miranda surveyed the skies around them. 'There he is.' She pointed towards a *very* small dot a *very* long way off.

'Come on, let's go and see Daddy.' Alice-Miranda set off at a gallop.

By the time the girls reached the paddock directly in front of the house, Cyril was manoeuvring Birdy in to land. Alice-Miranda and Jacinta waved furiously as they waited for the rotors to shut off. Chocolate curls flying, Alice-Miranda ran to greet her father who was out of the chopper and charging towards her. Hugh Kennington-Jones scooped his little daughter into his arms and gave her a smacking great kiss. The high pitched whine of the rotors suddenly gave way to silence as Birdy shuddered to a halt.

'Hello Jacinta, it's lovely to see you again.' Hugh put Alice-Miranda down and gave Jacinta an affectionate hug. 'I'm sorry I wasn't here this morning, girls, I had some urgent business in town. But now that's all done and I've brought someone home with me I'd like you to meet.'

'Who is it, Daddy?' Alice-Miranda peered back towards Birdy.

A tall man emerged from the helicopter. His tousled black hair matched his piercing dark eyes. He wore an emerald coloured jacket, well-fitting jeans and an extraordinary ruffled shirt which made him look a little like a pirate – albeit a very stylish one.

'Goodness.' Jacinta stared. 'Who's that?' she whispered behind her hand to Alice-Miranda.

Chapter 10

The man strode towards them, a chocolate leather overnight bag slung casually across his left shoulder. He placed it on the ground when he reached the group.

'Lawrence Ridley, this is my daughter Alice-Miranda and her friend Jacinta Headlington-Bear,' said Hugh.

'It's a pleasure to meet you, Mr Ridley.' Alice-Miranda offered him her tiny hand.

'And you too,' he nodded.

He offered his hand to Jacinta as well, which she shook vigorously.

'Your father has told me quite a lot about you, Alice-Miranda. It seems you are something of a matchmaker.' Mr Ridley smiled, revealing a picket fence row of dazzling white teeth.

'Daddy does go on,' Alice-Miranda replied. 'I just helped Mr Grump find his true love again. He was lost in the mountains, well not really lost, but he was lost because he didn't know what he wanted to do any more and then he told me all about his wife and how she was killed so tragically and then his daughter Amelia went to my school and he met Miss Grimm, my headmistress, and they fell in love but then Amelia got sick and it was all so sad—'

'Goodness, darling, you can take a breath,' her father interrupted.

'It's all right, Alice-Miranda – your father did mention something about you being quite the world champion talker too,' Lawrence joked.

Alice-Miranda rolled her eyes and grinned.

'Anyway, apparently I look just like Amelia and that was part of the reason Miss Grimm was so cross with me all the time but then Daddy sent Birdy to get Mr Grump and he and Mummy helped him get all cleaned up and then he came back to school and it was so romantic. They got married last month and Miss Grimm hasn't stopped smiling—'

'Are you famous?' Jacinta interrupted.

'Jacinta!' Alice-Miranda frowned at her friend.

'Well are you?' She wasn't about to give up. 'You look like someone. Someone I've seen in one of Mummy's magazines. Perhaps I've seen you at one of Mummy's parties – not that I get to go to them very often.'

'Well spotted, Jacinta,' said Hugh. He scooped Alice-Miranda onto his broad shoulders. 'Mr Ridley is an actor and a good friend of Aunt Charlotte's.'

'I knew I'd seen you somewhere before.' Jacinta grinned to herself, like a cat with a bowl of cream.

'Are you in films, Mr Ridley?' Alice-Miranda asked.

'I've done a few – romantic comedy, that sort of thing,' he replied.

'*Oh.*' Jacinta sounded like she was about to faint. 'Oh, oh, oh . . . you're . . . you're . . . Harry Winton! Well, not really Harry Winton because you're Lawrence Ridley but you *were* Harry Winton in *London Calling*. I love that movie, love, love, love it,' Jacinta gushed. 'It's my favourite ever!'

Lawrence's tanned face reddened. 'That's very kind of you, Jacinta.' He picked up his bag and the group began walking towards the house.

Hugh Kennington-Jones called back to the pilot. 'You can put Birdy away, Cyril, we won't need her again tonight. Thanks for today.'

'Very good, sir,' Cyril replied, as he hopped back into the chopper.

'Are you staying with us then, Mr Ridley?' Alice-Miranda asked.

'Yes,' her father answered. 'Mr Ridley will be our guest until the weekend.'

'Then you must tell us all about being a famous movie star.' Alice-Miranda held tight to her father's head. 'Is it terribly exciting?'

'Not as much as you'd think,' Lawrence replied.

'Well, I'm sure that we would love to hear about it just the same, wouldn't we, Jacinta?' Alice-Miranda glanced down at her friend, who had become rather quiet all of a sudden. 'Jacinta?' she called again.

Jacinta was gazing at Mr Ridley with a dreamy look on her face.

'Jacinta!' Alice-Miranda shouted.

'Yes, what? What did you say?' stammered Jacinta, blushing.

'I said that we'd love to know about Mr Ridley's acting, wouldn't we?' Alice-Miranda repeated.

'Yes, of course . . . love to.' Jacinta's already pink cheeks turned a deep scarlet.

Alice-Miranda leaned down and whispered into her father's ear, 'Daddy, do you think Jacinta has a crush?'

He glanced up at his daughter perched around his neck.

'Yes,' he whispered. 'I think you could be right.'

The group strode towards the house in the fading afternoon light. The sky was a palette of blue, high-lighted with purples and pinks.

'What a glorious sunset.' Lawrence stopped to take in the view. He turned 360 degrees, surveying the landscape in all directions. 'Splendid place you have here, Hugh – just beautiful.'

'Yes, it's pretty special.' Hugh lifted Alice-Miranda from his shoulders and set her back onto the ground. 'And it's all the better for having the girls home.' He smiled at his daughter and Jacinta.

'There's Mummy.' Alice-Miranda grabbed her father's hand. 'Come on.' She tugged his arm as she broke into a run.

'Look who we found,' Alice-Miranda exclaimed as they reached the porch where her mother was waiting.

'Hello, darling.' Hugh greeted Cecelia with a kiss.

'Lawrence!' she exclaimed, catching sight of him behind her husband. 'What a lovely surprise.' Cecelia hugged her guest and he kissed her on both cheeks. 'I hadn't realized you were coming down tonight. Charlotte thinks you're still in Paris filming. I've just got off the phone with her now.'

'It was the strangest thing,' said Hugh as he opened the front door for the group. 'I'd just finished my meeting at the club when who should I spy sitting around the corner in the lounge. Considering Lawrie was coming down for the weekend anyway, I asked if he wanted to have some extra days with us. And as luck would have it, he had his overnight bag with him just back from Paris.'

'I hope you don't mind, Cee.' Lawrence smiled his perfect smile.

'Of course not – it will be lovely to spend some time with you. I have a feeling we should be getting to know you a lot better,' Cecelia replied. 'Charlotte will be thrilled – she's coming down on

Friday, of course, but she might come earlier once she knows you're here.'

Lawrence put his bag down in the entrance hall. 'I'd rather not tell her just yet, if that's all right with you. There are a couple of things I'm trying to get organized and it will be impossible if she's here.' He winked at Cecelia. 'I'd like to surprise her.'

'Oh . . . oh, all right then.' Cecelia looked bemused. 'Girls – did you hear that? If Aunt Charlotte calls, you're not to tell her that we have a guest. It's our special secret, OK?'

Alice-Miranda and Jacinta nodded in agreement.

'Evening, Shilly,' Hugh Kennington-Jones greeted Mrs Shillingsworth as she entered the hallway and took his coat. 'Come and meet Mr Ridley. He's going to be our guest for the week.'

Mrs Shillingsworth frowned ever so slightly, then smiled and nodded at Mr Ridley. She knew there was no point being upset, as Mr Hugh had rather a habit of bringing friends home unannounced. And it wasn't as though they were short of room.

Hugh looked sheepish. 'I know – this is going to be such a busy week with all the preparations for the par—'

'Hugh!' Cecelia interrupted him. 'Why don't you

take Lawrence up to the blue room and I'll get the girls organized for dinner.' She turned around and raised her right index finger to her lips. The action was accompanied by what could only have been described as a meaningful look.

'Oh, of course, darling. Oops, almost let the cat—'

'Go!' Cecelia commanded.

'Mummy, what was Daddy going to say about cats?' Alice-Miranda gazed wide-eyed at her mother.

'Nothing, sweetheart, nothing at all. Now why don't you girls go upstairs and get cleaned up before dinner. Mrs Oliver has the most divine roast lamb on the go.'

'But Mummy, if it wasn't important why can't you tell us?' Alice-Miranda insisted.

'Just grown-up things,' her mother replied. 'Now off you go or you'll be late for dinner.'

'Come on, Jacinta.' Alice-Miranda bounded up the stairs with Jacinta close behind.

'Do you think your parents are getting you a cat?' Jacinta asked.

'I can't imagine. Mummy's allergic to cat fur and the only cats allowed live in the stables,' said Alice-Miranda, shaking her head.

* * *

Back in the hallway, Mrs Shillingsworth was also shaking her head.

'I should have known he might say something,' said Cecelia, with her hands on her hips. 'He can never keep a secret and I want the girls to get a surprise. But isn't it lovely that Lawrence can spend some time with us?' she asked.

The two women walked through to the sitting room where Shilly began to prepare a drinks tray. She gathered crystal tumblers from a decorative Regency cabinet and set them on a silver tray. Cecelia disappeared to the kitchen and reappeared a few minutes later with a jug of water and a bucket of ice.

'I'm sorry about the extra work, Shilly,' Cecelia apologised as she set the jug and bucket on the sideboard. 'You know Hugh can't help himself when it comes to guests. And he is rather gorgeous, isn't he?' Cecelia raised her arched eyebrows.

'Who, ma'am?' Shilly asked remotely, trying to be cross. She wasn't very good at it.

'Mr Ridley, of course,' Cecelia replied. 'I think Charlotte's a very lucky girl.'

Shilly tried to suppress a smile but then giggled like a schoolgirl. 'Well, I don't think I mind *too* much. I think it's those eyes – impossibly dark, aren't they? Ever since Dolly and I watched that movie, you know the one where he pretends to be a writer in France – he sends all those love letters. What was it called again?' Shilly dropped an ice cube into one of the glasses. It tinkled loudly against the crystal.

'*Letters from Lyon*.' Lawrence suddenly appeared in the doorway.

'That was quick!' Cecelia spun around.

'Sorry – I shouldn't have been listening,' he apologised.

'Very good, sir,' Shilly whispered, her cheeks lighting up the room. 'I'd better attend to the table,' she muttered, bustling off. 'Small dining room tonight, ma'am.'

'There's no need to go to any trouble,' Cecelia called. 'We'd be happy to eat in the kitchen with you and Dolly.'

But Shilly had gone.

'Lawrence, you naughty thing,' Cecelia admonished. 'Poor Shilly won't be able to look at you again.'

'Sorry, Cee – I only heard the part about the movie. Thought I'd help her out.'

'She was telling me how much she admired your work, among other things,' Cecelia added.

'Oh. I'll see what I can do to put her at ease,' Lawrence offered.

'Come on, then, let's have a drink before dinner.' Cecelia linked her arm into Lawrence's and led him across the room.

Chapter 11

The family was seated around a rectangular mahogany table in the small dining room, adjacent to the kitchens. The main dining hall at the front of the house was reserved for formal occasions only. With a table for one hundred and two, they had little use for it on a daily basis. The family usually ate with Mrs Oliver and Shilly in the kitchen but the unexpected arrival of Lawrence Ridley had prompted Mrs Shillingsworth to move the evening meal to the dining room instead. That and her fear of having to face him again after their earlier encounter.

Dinner had been a mostly happy affair. Amid the chinking of glasses and cutlery, Alice-Miranda talked non-stop about school and all the things she had done in the past term. Hugh and Cecelia were so pleased to have her home that they hadn't stopped smiling. Jacinta spent the entire meal gazing at Mr Ridley, which to begin with he found quite sweet, but after a while thought somewhat unnerving.

'That was delicious,' Alice-Miranda enthused as Mrs Oliver appeared and began clearing the plates. 'You know, I think your roast lamb is my absolute favourite. And that cauliflower cheese was superb – there's no one who makes it like you do. Mrs Smith does try but it's just not there yet – but please don't tell her I said so. I would hate to hurt her feelings.' Alice-Miranda began to stand. 'Would you like some help cleaning up?'

'No thank you, darling girl. Shilly was coming but she seems to have disappeared,' Mrs Oliver frowned.

'I'll give you a hand, Dolly.' Hugh rose from his seat at the head of the table and gathered up his and Lawrence's plates.

'Thank you, sir,' she nodded.

'You know, your Mrs Oliver reminds me of someone.' Lawrence frowned as Dolly and Hugh left the room.

'She looks just like Mummy's godmother, Aunty Gee,' Alice-Miranda offered.

'Would I know your Aunty Gee?' Lawrence quizzed.

'You might have seen her once or twice,' Cecelia teased.

'So, what's it really like being an actor, Mr Ridley?' said Alice-Miranda, focusing on their guest. 'Is it very exciting and glamorous? Do you get to meet lots of other actors and have amazing adventures all over the place?'

Lawrence wiped a minuscule spot of gravy from his lip and folded his napkin neatly on the table. 'I'd say it has its moments,' he began. 'There are some very exciting parts and then quite a lot of not-so-exciting parts. We spend a great deal of time rehearsing, then one scene can take days to film depending on how many takes there are. And then when you're not involved in anything you tend to spend quite a while playing cards with whoever else is at a loose end.'

'That doesn't sound very glamorous at all, does it Jacinta?' Alice-Miranda turned to her friend, who was staring doe-eyed at Mr Ridley.

'Yes, glamorous . . .' Jacinta sighed.

Alice-Miranda giggled.

Hugh Kennington-Jones reappeared carrying a tray of steaming chocolate puddings. Mrs Oliver was close behind with a jug of cream. She followed Hugh around the table setting the bowls down and pouring cream onto the puddings, which were nestled beside a dollop of ice-cream.

'That smells amazing.' Alice-Miranda raised her button nose into the air and drew in a deep breath.

'Join us, Dolly?' Hugh motioned towards the empty seat beside Mr Ridley.

'Thank you, sir, but if it's all the same, I've made some rather exciting progress downstairs and I'm very eager to continue.' She nodded her head, barely suppressing a satisfied smile.

'That sounds interesting. Mind if I pop down later?' Hugh asked.

'Perhaps if you wait until next week, I'll have more to show you,' Dolly replied.

'You just let me know when I can have a look,' Hugh asked. 'Now leave *us* to do the kitchen. I'm sure cleaning up will be a novelty for the girls.' Hugh winked at Alice-Miranda.

'Very well, sir,' said Dolly. She turned and bustled out of the room.

Lawrence was confused. 'Progress? Downstairs? What was she talking about?'

Hugh's face mirrored that of a proud parent. 'Well, Lawrence, you see our Dolly is not only the most brilliant cook, she's also something of a scientist. Years ago, Cee's father set her up with a laboratory in the cellars and since then she has made amazing discoveries. I'm not entirely sure what she's up to at the moment. You know she perfected FDF miniaturisation earlier in the year?'

'FDF?' Lawrence frowned.

'Freeze-Dried Foods,' Alice-Miranda replied. 'We're all trying to come up with a better name for it when it goes into production. FDF is a bit dull. Anyway, Mrs Oliver started with baked dinners – they're so delicious you really can't tell the difference between them and what we had tonight. I ate them for three nights when I was on my hike last term,' she enthused. 'And they hardly weigh a thing so you can carry days' worth of food without even thinking about it.'

'Might I have read something about that in the paper a little while ago?' Lawrence asked. 'I mean, freeze-drying is nothing new but this article made out that you could, um, what was it, just add water to a handful of beans and, hey presto, you've got yourself a baked dinner?'

'Yes, that's right. There was a small article in *The Times*,' Hugh replied. 'But the chap writing it was something of a cynic, and he made it all sound like the stuff of science fiction.'

'Mrs Oliver has invented lots of other FDF recipes – she's so clever,' Alice-Miranda nodded.

'And now we're working with Care Planet to get government distribution contracts,' her father added.

'Really?' Lawrence said thoughtfully. 'And she does all that in the cellar here' – he took a mouthful of pudding – 'on your time?'

'Dolly's not just an employee,' Hugh rebuked. He thrust his spoon into the pudding, spewing a splodge of ice-cream over the side of the bowl and onto the tablecloth.

'Well, I imagine her invention hasn't made her very popular with some of the Third World bureaucrats,' Lawrence went on, seemingly oblivious to the distaste of his host.

Hugh swallowed deliberately. 'I don't think any of us cares about whether the local authorities like it,' he retorted. 'As long as there's a water supply, which tends to be the most difficult part of the whole equation, it will work. I think Dolly has made one of the most important discoveries the world has known. We have teams out building wells all over the place, but there's a lot of red tape.'

'Must be costing you a bomb,' Lawrence observed. 'I hope the old bird cuts you some of the action.'

Alice-Miranda looked at her father, then at Mr Ridley as their conversation ricocheted back and forth across the table.

'That is actually none of your business, Lawrence,' Hugh snapped. 'I think this has more to do with giving people a better quality of life. I couldn't care less about the money.'

Lawrence looked sheepish. 'Don't get me wrong, Hugh. It's just that when I was filming in Africa last year it seemed to me that corruption was a way of life in many places. I'd have thought some governments would have been just as happy to see the starving stay that way.'

'Is that true, Daddy?' Alice-Miranda asked.

'Unfortunately, sweetheart, Mr Ridley is right – *about that.* There are governments who stay in power because they control pretty much everything. Including people's access to food, housing, education and medical care,' her father said, before shovelling another spoonful of pudding into his mouth.

'That's horrible,' Jacinta added, her attention turning from Mr Ridley for the first time since they had sat down.

'Well, I'm sure there'd be more than a few people who'd like to get their hands on your Mrs Oliver's formulas. I hope she has them locked up tight,' Lawrence continued.

'She keeps it all up here.' Hugh tapped his temple.

Lawrence looked aghast. 'What? Nothing written down? That's a bit risky.'

'Perhaps some basics, but I know the secret ingredients are safely secured in Dolly's head. It's likely she has them somewhere else, but she's never told me,' Hugh replied.

'Well, I hope nothing happens to the old girl. That'd be a disaster,' Lawrence added.

'Nothing's going to happen to Dolly.' Hugh slammed his spoon down onto the table. 'She's as tough as old boots and as clever as a cat. No doubt there's a contingency plan somewhere – Cee and I will hear about it when we need to,' Hugh replied, fiddling with the corner of his napkin. An uneasy silence hovered in the room.

Aware of her husband's discomfort, Cecelia attempted to change the subject. 'So tell us, girls, what did you get up to this afternoon?'

'Look Hugh, I didn't mean anything by that,' Lawrence apologized.

Hugh glanced across at his wife, then back to their guest. 'Yes, well, I suppose the whole situation is a little unusual,' he replied as the frown lines on his forehead began to smooth out. 'It's just that Dolly's a member of the family, Lawrence. Her work is important to all of us.'

Lawrence nodded.

'Sorry darling,' said Hugh, turning to Alice-Miranda. 'Mummy asked what you girls got up to today and we didn't let you get a word in.'

'Well, we had the most wonderful time. First we went to see Jasper and Poppy. Then we all went together to visit Daisy and Granny Bert,' Alice-Miranda began.

'Then we had afternoon tea with the Greenings,' Jacinta continued.

'And we met that boy, Mummy, the one in the laneway,' Alice-Miranda added.

'Yes, that *awful* boy,' Jacinta emphasised. 'He was in one of the oak trees in the field and he pelted us with stones. Then he pushed Alice-Miranda over.' Jacinta was *still* indignant on her friend's behalf.

'A boy?' Lawrence looked at Jacinta. 'Where did he come from?'

'Well, I don't really know exactly. Poppy said that he belongs to them because his mother doesn't want him any more,' Alice-Miranda explained. 'But that just sounds too awful for words. Imagine, not being wanted.'

'Does this boy have a name?' Lawrence asked.

'Lucasss,' Jacinta hissed.

'Oh,' Lawrence nodded. 'Awful you say?'

'Yes, he's a total brat,' Jacinta proclaimed.

'I wouldn't say that, Jacinta. We really don't know him at all. Do you know anything about him, Mummy?' Alice-Miranda asked, turning to her mother.

'Well, if his name's Lucas then he's Lily's nephew, darling. I don't know much about him either, other than that he came to stay a couple of weeks ago. I haven't had a moment to meet him yet. But if he pushed you over, I will have a word to her tomorrow,' her mother added.

'It's all right. He didn't hurt me,' Alice-Miranda protested. 'There was something about him, something sad.'

'How do you mean?' Lawrence asked.

'Well I think he's sad because underneath all that toughness, he's just angry and upset. If it's true that his mother doesn't want him, then really, who would blame the poor boy for being that way? That's awful. I don't want him to get into trouble,' Alice-Miranda reassured her parents. 'You know I can look after myself.'

If there was one thing they most certainly did know, it was that their daughter was more than capable of looking after her own affairs. After the term she had just had, they were convinced more than ever that she really was a most capable child.

Chapter 12

That night, Alice-Miranda lay in her bed thinking about her day. She had been looking forward to coming home and it was so lovely to see everyone. But there was something bothering her. Not anything in particular, just a strange feeling that things weren't quite right. And Alice-Miranda had a very good nose for strange feelings.

Lying in her enormous bed, she felt awfully small.

Alice-Miranda stared at the canopy above her, fighting off the sleep that threatened to interrupt the film of the day she was replaying in her head. There had been lots of lovely things but she was worried about Lucas. And then Daisy was upset too, but she wouldn't say why. There was that strange black car in the laneway and then Mr Ridley arrived. He was very friendly and terribly handsome, but he had argued with Daddy at dinner and that had given her a bad feeling.

Her eyelids were getting heavier and her mind was drifting when the door to her bathroom flew open and Jacinta leaped onto her bed.

Alice-Miranda sat bolt upright. 'What? What is it?'

'I need you to see something,' Jacinta whispered loudly.

'What's the matter?' Alice-Miranda's brown eyes were at once wide and alert.

'I just saw Mr Ridley in the garden.'

'What were you doing in the garden?' Alice-Miranda asked.

'Come on, I'll show you.' Jacinta pulled back the covers and grabbed Alice-Miranda's arm.

She opened the bedroom door and leaned her head outside, then turned back to her friend. 'Clear!'

On bare toes, the girls crept along the hallway to the top of the staircase.

'I think we should use the kitchen stairs.' Alice-Miranda tugged Jacinta's arm and motioned towards the other end of the hall. 'It's quieter than the foyer and we don't want to wake up the whole house, although Daddy seems to have bionic hearing and sleeps with one eye open.' She giggled until Jacinta hushed her with a fierce look.

'Then *stop* talking!' Jacinta hissed. 'What about Mrs Oliver and Shilly?'

'Most likely in bed.' Alice-Miranda pointed at the grandfather clock that stood on the landing halfway down the main staircase. It was about to strike twelve.

The girls made their way along the hall, anxious that every step could be their undoing. Old houses had a way of giving up their secrets at the most inopportune times; they listened for every creak and groan and tiptoed down the kitchen stairs.

A light flickered as they reached the bottom and Alice-Miranda realized that it was the television in the side sitting room. She pressed her finger to her lips and started across the kitchen floor. There was a loud grunt, and a snort. Alice-Miranda jumped as she realized that Shilly was sitting in her favourite armchair. The girls froze. And then there was a sound like air escaping from a balloon. Jacinta stifled a laugh. Shilly began snoring very loudly.

The girls reached the outside kitchen door and Alice-Miranda gently turned the handle. It wasn't locked. They never were. On the side porch the girls allowed their eyes to adjust to the light. A golden moon hung in a pillow of clouds, gently illuminating the garden around them. The sky was scattered with diamonds.

'Where did you see him?' Alice-Miranda whispered.

Jacinta pointed towards the walled garden.

The girls crept around the veranda, eager to avoid the crunchy gravel driveway. When they reached the grass, Alice-Miranda grabbed Jacinta by the hand and they shot off into the garden – in search of what exactly, Alice-Miranda still did not really know.

They reached the cherub fountain and at last Alice-Miranda felt it was safe to talk.

'What's going on?' she demanded.

Jacinta's eyes were wide with excitement. 'I couldn't sleep, so I thought I would do some stretching on the floor in my bedroom. But then I heard a door click and I thought it might have been you so I peeked outside for a better look. But it wasn't you, it was Mr Ridley and he was wearing a black cloak and carrying a yellow folder. He was checking to see that there was no one in the hallway so I quickly ducked my head back inside and waited until he had gone. Then I followed him and he went downstairs and out the front door. I was a bit worried about going after him in the dark on my own, so I ran back to the bedroom to see if I could track where he went from the window.'

'He probably couldn't sleep like you, and me too now,' Alice-Miranda replied.

'That's what I thought to begin with but then I saw a light coming from the field beyond the walled garden. And then there was an outline of a figure. He was meeting someone.'

Alice-Miranda's mind began to race. Who would he be meeting in the middle of the night? Didn't Daddy say that it was just a coincidence that he ran into Mr Ridley at the club? It was rather strange.

'What do you think he's doing?' Jacinta sounded a little worried – but mostly excited now.

'I don't know.' Alice-Miranda bit her lip. 'Perhaps we should go and see if we can find him?' She took

Jacinta's hand and they scurried to the door in the stone wall, which led through to the long meadow. Alice-Miranda was about to turn the brass handle when they heard voices. They were getting closer. Jacinta grabbed Alice-Miranda's hand and wrenched her behind a nearby camellia hedge.

The handle turned. Alice-Miranda began to stand up when Jacinta pulled her arm and she fell with a thump onto the lawn.

'What did you do that for?' asked Alice-Miranda as she dusted herself off and kneeled on the ground.

'Sorry,' Jacinta mouthed. 'I don't think you should go out there. What if he's up to no good?'

Alice-Miranda was not convinced. Jacinta kneeled up too and tried to part the leaves to get a better look, but there was too much foliage. The girls had to rely on their ears instead.

'Thank you,' came Lawrence's voice. 'This is worth more to me than gold.'

The other voice sounded like a woman's. If the speakers took just a few more steps into the garden, the girls might have heard better.

Jacinta screwed up her nose and looked at Alice-Miranda, who was shaking her head. Neither of them could work out what the woman was saying.

'I'd better get back,' Lawrence whispered. 'Don't want anyone to miss me.'

'. . . maybe tomorrow or the next day . . .' was all Alice-Miranda could make out from the female voice.

'Just let me know . . .' Lawrence closed the door and swept back towards the house.

Alice-Miranda popped up first, followed by Jacinta.

'What was all that?'

'"Worth more than gold?" I wonder what he was talking about?' Alice-Miranda had a twisting feeling in her stomach. 'We'd better get back to the house.'

The girls walked to the edge of the garden and waited until they saw Lawrence disappearing though the front door and up the stairs.

Back in the safety of Alice-Miranda's bedroom, the pair lay side by side whispering about what they had just seen and heard.

'You should tell your parents in the morning.' Jacinta pulled the covers up under her chin.

'Why don't we just ask Mr Ridley?' Alice-Miranda suggested.

'But what if he's up to no good?' Jacinta replied. 'He's probably a spy or something – he did seem to know lots of things about African governments at dinner time.' She gasped. 'Oh, how romantic.'

Alice-Miranda made up her mind. 'Well, I'm going to talk to him as soon as I can. Perhaps I could go now. I'm sure there is a perfectly good explanation for his midnight meeting.' She glanced at the clock beside her bed. It was almost 1 a.m. – perhaps a bit late to be bothering their guest. 'Do you want to stay here tonight?' she asked, turning to her friend. But Jacinta was already fast asleep.

Chapter 13

Alice-Miranda was awake early. She had dreamed of all manner of strange things and it took her a minute to remember that their nocturnal adventure into the garden had in fact actually happened. Jacinta was still asleep. Her delicate even breaths were occasionally punctuated by loud grunts that would rival Shilly's best efforts. Alice-Miranda was impressed.

Not wanting to wake her, Alice-Miranda grabbed a clean shirt, a pair of socks and the jeans that were hanging over the back of her chair and crept to the bathroom. She dressed quickly and exited through Jacinta's adjoining room.

She was determined to have a chat with Mr Ridley before the whole house was awake.

Tiptoeing along the hallway to the blue room, Alice-Miranda raised her tiny hand and knocked ever so gently. From inside she thought she could hear papers rustling so she knocked again – a little harder. She waited, just a moment, and then turned the handle.

'Mr Ridley, are you there? It's me, Alice-Miranda,' she announced. 'I wondered if we could have a quick chat?' She leaned around the door to take a peek inside. The four-poster bed was empty and unmade. The curtains were billowing and there were papers scattered all over the floor.

Alice-Miranda climbed up onto the writing table to shut the window. She pulled hard. The giant frame squeaked and shuddered as she hauled with all her might. It finally released and hit the sill with a thud. Alice-Miranda snipped the brass latch before attempting to push the curtains back behind the desk as best she could manage.

There was a yellow folder on the floor – perhaps it was the same one Jacinta had seen Mr Ridley carrying last night. Alice-Miranda wasn't going to look at the papers; she knew it was wrong to mind other people's private business. But Shilly would have a fit if she saw the mess. Anyway, they looked like handwritten letters and she still wasn't very good at reading fancy curly-swirly writing. Alice-Miranda shuffled the pages back together and was about to place them in the folder when something caught her eye – a name at the bottom of one of the papers.

Kitty. Now, where had she heard that name lately? And then she remembered. What a strange coincidence, she thought. Her mind began to race. Perhaps Lawrence's meeting her father in the club yesterday afternoon wasn't just an accident after all.

Alice-Miranda placed the folder on the writing table and promptly left the room.

She scampered down the kitchen stairs, hoping to find Mr Ridley at breakfast. Mrs Oliver was bustling about stirring pots and buttering toast. The scrubbed table was set for five but Alice-Miranda noticed that two spots were already playing host to dirty bowls and plates.

'Hello, my darling girl.' Dolly turned from the steaming pot of porridge simmering on the stove. 'You're up bright and early. Jacinta still asleep?'

'Yes, I didn't want to wake her. I mean, it is holiday after all,' Alice-Miranda pulled out a chair and sat down. 'Have Daddy and Mummy had breakfast already?' she asked, surveying the empty plates opposite.

'No, it was your father and Mr Ridley up early. Shilly and I were having a quiet start to the day, enjoying some tea and toast with a rather thick helping of Mrs Smith's cherry jam, might I add, when they clattered downstairs. I don't know what happened last night but Shilly turned the colour of those apples there' – Mrs Oliver pointed at the bowl of Red Delicious in the middle of the table – 'and immediately made an excuse that she needed to start on polishing the silver in the dining room. At this hour. Can you imagine? Anyway, they've gone for a ride and I don't think they plan to be back for quite some time. Your father mentioned something about lunch at the Red Lion so goodness knows when they'll return.'

'Oh.' Alice-Miranda's tone betrayed her disappointment.

'But your father said that when he gets back he will give you girls his undivided attention,' Dolly continued. 'He wanted to let you sleep in on your first morning home. Now, what would you like for your breakfast?'

'Umm . . . scrambled eggs please,' Alice-Miranda replied. 'If that's not too much trouble. I can have porridge if it's easier,' she added.

'Get off with you, young lady. You know it's no bother and if the day should arrive that it were, I would find myself a cottage and move there in the morn,' Dolly quipped. 'Now sit down and pour yourself some of that juice. Mr Greening picked those oranges just yesterday.'

Alice-Miranda filled a tumbler.

At that moment Cecelia Highton-Smith appeared on the stairs. She was dressed for action, as she would call it, in jeans and a pinstriped long-sleeved shirt. Alice-Miranda knew this could mean only one thing – some or other room was about to get the once-over.

'Morning darling.' Cecelia kissed the top of Alice-Miranda's head and sat down opposite her. 'You're up early. I thought you and Jacinta would like a sleep-in. I can always remember the best part of coming home for the holidays was not being woken by that wretched bell.'

Alice-Miranda explained that Jacinta was still asleep but she had hoped to catch Mr Ridley this morning. There was something she wanted to ask him.

'Darling, please don't badger Lawrence. I imagine he spends a great deal of his life bombarded with cameras and questions. Can you think what it must be like to live every minute of your life in the spotlight?' Cecelia lectured.

'Of course, Mummy. But . . . how well does Aunt Charlotte know Mr Ridley?' Alice-Miranda asked.

'Darling, I'm sure that she would prefer to tell you herself, but seeing that she's not here – I think that they are very much in love.'

'But how long has Aunt Charlotte known Mr Ridley?' Alice-Miranda asked before taking a sip of juice.

'I think about six months. But that doesn't really matter, does it? When it's right, you just know,' Cecelia smiled.

Alice-Miranda decided then not to tell her mother and father about what she and Jacinta had seen the previous night. She would rather talk to Mr Ridley herself and anyway, she didn't know for sure that he was doing anything wrong. Her parents would only worry and she didn't want to cause a fuss if there was nothing to fuss about. And surely there wasn't.

'What are you doing today, Mummy?' Alice-Miranda asked as Mrs Oliver placed a plate of creamy scrambled eggs on hot buttered toast in front of her.

'I'm afraid I have rather a lot of work to do. Daisy's coming over and we're going to attack the dining room. I think Shilly has asked Mrs Greening to give us a hand too and there are some lads coming up from the village, so I won't be much fun. Why don't you and Jacinta see what Poppy and Jasper are up to?' Her mother poured herself a cup of tea from the silver pot on the table.

Managing a house the size of Highton Hall demanded strict schedules and almost continuous rosters of dusting, polishing, vacuuming and other maintenance. Alice-Miranda was used to the fact that at least once a week, under Shilly's military-like command, her mother and Daisy could be found leading the cleaning charge. Cecelia often put her slim figure and stamina down to the never-ending household chores.

'Is Lily helping too?' Alice-Miranda asked, wondering if perhaps she could shed any light on the mystery of Mr Ridley's midnight meeting.

'No, darling, I think Lily's got other things on her mind.'

'The village lads don't usually come unless there's something special happening,' Alice-Miranda noted, glancing up at her mother.

'Nothing special darling. It's just that Daddy and I have been away quite a lot this last month, so things have been a little neglected. Daisy's been busy taking care of Granny Bert and Lily has had her hands full too, so we just need to catch up,' Cecelia replied innocently. Alice-Miranda was not convinced.

At that moment Jacinta plodded downstairs.

'Good morning,' Cecelia, Alice-Miranda and Mrs Oliver chorused.

'Hello, everyone.' Jacinta stretched her arms and yawned. 'Oh, *excuse* me. I don't know why I'm still tired. I slept like a cat.' A tickle pounced on the tip of Jacinta's nose and suddenly she sneezed loudly.

'Bless you, my girl,' said Dolly.

'That doesn't sound too good. I hope you're not coming down with something, Jacinta. Come and have breakfast.' Cecelia motioned to Jacinta to take her place at the table. 'What would you like to eat? You can have anything you want.'

'Goodness,' Jacinta sighed. 'That does give me rather a lot of options.' She spied Alice-Miranda's half-eaten scrambled eggs. 'May I have the same as Alice-Miranda please?' she asked, then yawned again.

'Good choice. Mrs Oliver makes the best scrambled eggs ever,' Alice-Miranda enthused.

'Did you tell your mother about Mr Ridley?' Jacinta asked, lowering her voice conspiratorially.

'What about Mr Ridley, darling?' Cecelia raised her left eyebrow.

Alice-Miranda shot Jacinta a knowing look. 'Mr Ridley's very handsome, isn't he, Mummy?'

'Yes, darling. He is,' her mother agreed. 'Is that all?'

'That's all.' Alice-Miranda didn't like keeping things from her mother but she really didn't want to cause a bother. She shook her head at Jacinta, who was about to say something else.

'You are a funny little thing sometimes,' her mother laughed.

Mrs Oliver placed Jacinta's perfect scrambled eggs in front of her. Cecelia finished her tea and nibbled at a piece of jam toast while she read the paper.

'What do you want to do today?' Alice-Miranda asked her guest.

'I don't mind,' Jacinta replied. 'Maybe we should go and see Jasper and Poppy. And remember you promised to take Granny Bert for a wheel around the garden – I just hope she's in a better mood.'

'Granny Bert in a better mood?' Mrs Oliver turned from the steaming sink where she was scrubbing a large frypan. 'You're an optimist if ever I've heard one.'

'We'll go straight after breakfast,' said Alice-Miranda. She stood and carried her plate to the sink. 'And hopefully Daddy and Mr Ridley will be back just after lunch.'

'Thank you, darling girl.' Mrs Oliver took the dirty dishes and began to stack them in the dish-washer. 'Now why don't you run along and brush your teeth and I will pack a picnic for your lunch. How does that sound?'

'Brilliant!' Alice-Miranda gave Dolly a quick hug. 'See you in a minute,' she called to Jacinta.

She bounded upstairs leaving her mother and Jacinta to finish their breakfast. Cecelia was as unconvinced by her daughter's earlier answer as Alice-Miranda was of her explanation on the subject of the cleaning. She decided Jacinta might be a more reliable source.

'Jacinta, what did you mean before about Mr Ridley? Is there something I should know?' She folded the newspaper and set it to the side.

'No, not at all,' Jacinta replied, a little too quickly for Cecelia's liking. 'Alice-Miranda and I were just talking last night about how gorgeous Mr Ridley is. No wonder he's a movie star,' she raved. 'Those eyes are soooo dreamy. If only I was ten years older.' She sighed dramatically.

'Yes, he is quite something,' Cecelia agreed. Jacinta's response satisfied her curiosity for the moment. She had a lot of things on her mind and besides, Hugh had taken Lawrence out for a ride and she doubted they would be back for hours. Their guest was safe for a little while at least.

Chapter 14

By the time the girls headed off, Jacinta had sneezed another twelve times. Her voice was beginning to croak and Cecelia was worried that she was getting sick. Despite not feeling one hundred per cent, Jacinta insisted on carrying the delicious spread Dolly had packed for them.

'If you start to feel worse Jacinta, please come home,' Cecelia insisted. 'We can tuck you up in bed with a pile of books and some tea and crumpets.'

Jacinta didn't want to admit it but that sounded rather good. She hated being ill and it was just her luck to come down with something in the holidays – again. But this time the pleasure of having someone as warm and patient and lovely as Mrs Oliver or Cecelia looking after her was rather more appealing than she was prepared to confess.

'We'll go and find Poppy and Jasper first. Maybe we can go for a walk to the stream. And we have an amazing cubby – it's totally hidden.'

'Aaah-choo,' Jacinta sneezed again and shivered miserably. She didn't want to disappoint Alice-Miranda but as always her little friend knew just the right thing to say.

'Bless you. Are you sure you want to go at all?'

'I might feel better for a walk and' – she turned to face Alice-Miranda and mouthed silently – '*we have to talk about you know what.*' Jacinta picked up the pack and hauled it onto her shoulder.

The two girls set off across the lawn towards the walled garden and the scene of the previous night's mystery meeting.

'We should keep an eye out for clues,' Jacinta suggested. 'Perhaps Mr Ridley dropped something while he was out here last night.'

'I went to see him this morning before you woke up,' said Alice-Miranda.

Jacinta stopped and turned to face her friend. 'What did he say?'

'He wasn't there. The window was open and the breeze had scattered papers all over the floor. I picked them up,' Alice-Miranda began.

'And?' Jacinta gripped Alice-Miranda's hands tightly.

'Well, I didn't look at anything on purpose, because it's wrong to pry into other people's private things, but there was a letter. I couldn't help seeing it.'

'What did it say?' Jacinta shook Alice-Miranda's arms.

'I didn't read it.'

'Why not?' Jacinta demanded.

'I couldn't! That would be very bad manners. But I did see who it was from.'

'Who?' Jacinta was practically bursting.

'I'm pretty sure it said Kitty.'

'Who's Kitty?'

'I don't know for sure. But didn't Jasper say something about Aunty Kitty yesterday when we were asking about Lucas?' Alice-Miranda replied.

'Yes, he did. Mr Ridley must be up to something,' Jacinta insisted. 'It's all too much of a coincidence him meeting your father by accident at the club. I can't believe that he just happened to meet someone out here in the middle of the night by accident too.' She shook her head in disbelief.

'I don't know. I'll talk to him as soon as I can. But for now I think we should just go and find Jasper and Poppy and enjoy our first proper day of holidays.'

Alice-Miranda looked at her friend, who answered with a very loud *aah-choo!* 'Bless you again,' Alice-Miranda smiled.

'All right. But you must admit, it's pretty exciting, for me anyway.' Jacinta frowned. 'It's not every day you get to stay in the same place as a real live movie star, and especially not one as handsome and mysterious as Lawrence Ridley,' she gushed.

'That's true. Oh, look.' Alice-Miranda pointed towards the barn near Rose Cottage. 'There's Jasper – let's see if he wants to play.' She began to run.

Alice-Miranda called out to Jasper as they neared the building. He had his back to the girls and as they drew closer they could hear shouting.

'You've wrecked everything. It took me forever to put this together and look what you've done.'

He rushed forward into the shadows, his fists pummelling.

'Jasper,' Alice-Miranda called.

This time he swivelled around. 'Go away!' he yelled.

Jacinta caught up to Alice-Miranda and as their eyes adjusted to the light, the girls saw that Lucas was standing in the shadow against the barn wall, the object of Jasper's anger.

'Oh look – so sweet – your little girlfriend's come to save you,' Lucas sneered.

'Shut up,' Jasper yelled. 'She's *not* my girlfriend.'

'Hello, Jasper. Hello, Lucas,' Alice-Miranda interrupted. 'Is there something the matter?'

'He's wrecked everything – as usual,' Jasper fumed.

'It was only a stupid model.' Lucas's black eyes glinted in the half light. 'You've got hundreds of them. And it's not wrecked – you just have to repaint it.'

'Look!' Jasper demanded, holding out the miniature tank which appeared to be missing its tracks. 'I've been working on this for weeks and it's ruined.'

'Gee, you're getting a bit worked up aren't you? It's only a toy,' Lucas smirked.

'May I have a look?' Alice-Miranda reached out and Jasper reluctantly gave her the model. 'It does look a bit worse for wear.' She gently turned it around in her hands. 'Maybe you could fix it,' she suggested to Lucas.

'Yeah and maybe you could *drop dead!*' he yelled.

'Lucas, that's really not very nice,' Alice-Miranda replied.

'I told you yesterday, I'm *not* very nice. And I really don't feel the need to be *nice* to you.' Lucas snatched the model from Alice-Miranda's hands and threw it to the ground. Then he proceeded to jump up and down on it until it was smashed beyond recognition. Jasper, Alice-Miranda and Jacinta stood staring, their mouths gaping like a choir of singing codfish. Lucas reached down and picked it up, then thrust it towards Jasper.

'I didn't wreck it in the first place but since I'm going to get the blame for everything around here, just like at that stupid school . . .' He shoved Alice-Miranda out of the way and stormed around the corner of the barn, disappearing from sight.

'Monster,' Jacinta shouted after him.

Jasper examined the ruined model, then looked at Alice-Miranda. 'Why did you have to butt in?'

'I was just trying to help.' Alice-Miranda patted his shoulder.

Jasper flinched. 'I didn't need your help. Look what you did – at least before it could be fixed. Now it's totally wrecked.' His voice quivered and the moisture in his eyes threatened to spill. 'Just go back to that dumb school and leave me alone,' he cried and ran towards the house.

'I guess that means Jasper doesn't want to come on the picnic,' Jacinta croaked.

'No, I suppose not,' Alice-Miranda replied thoughtfully. She had never seen Jasper so upset before, and Lucas – she couldn't believe there was anyone in the world even angrier than Alethea Goldsworthy. Alice-Miranda made up her mind that she should talk to Lily as soon as she had the chance. Jacinta sneezed, *ah-choo, ah-choo, ah-choo*. Her nose was red and despite the warm morning she had started to shiver.

'You look terrible,' said Alice-Miranda, realizing that Jacinta was really unwell. 'We should go home and get you to bed.'

Jacinta felt terrible.

'It's not fair,' she said, plodding along beside her friend. 'I hate being sick.'

'Not to worry.' Alice-Miranda squeezed Jacinta's hand. 'You just need a rest, that's all, and I'm sure you'll be better in no time.'

'Maybe if I sleep today I will be better by tomorrow and then we can have some proper adventures,' Jacinta said sulkily. 'I don't want to miss anything.'

Alice-Miranda realized that having some time to herself was exactly what was needed. She planned to talk to Lily, then find Lucas and see if he would apologize to Jasper. The last thing she wanted was for Jasper to be upset.

The girls reached the kitchen and found Mrs Oliver writing some notes in her special cookbook.

'Oh dear me!' she exclaimed as she caught sight of Jacinta and her ruby nose. 'You two didn't get far.'

Jacinta promptly dropped the backpack on the kitchen floor and answered with another three loud sneezes.

'Bless you and bless you and bless you again,' Mrs Oliver replied.

She strode into the pantry and produced two of her special tonics which she measured into two medicine glasses. 'This one's for you, Miss Jacinta – it will ease the sniffles and sneezes.' She handed Jacinta a glass of blue potion. 'And this, darling girl, is for you – stop a bull in its tracks it will.'

Alice-Miranda took a swig of the green goop and shuddered. 'That's disgusting.' She pulled a face.

Jacinta swallowed, anticipating an equally terrible taste. 'That's lovely,' she cooed. 'It's the best tasting medicine I've ever had.'

'Why does this one taste so bad?' Alice-Miranda asked as she placed the empty glass down onto the table.

'My apologies.' Mrs Oliver popped the corks back into the bottles. 'I'm still working on an acceptable flavour – just can't seem to get it right.'

'This one tastes like honey and chocolate and crisp green apples all rolled into one,' said Jacinta, licking her lips.

'Well, this one tastes like pond scum.' Alice-Miranda poured herself a large glass of water from the tap and swished it around in her mouth.

'And how would you know what pond scum tastes like, my girl?' Mrs Oliver asked, her eyes smiling.

'It smells like it,' Alice-Miranda replied, 'so I imagine that's what it tastes like too. But I'm sure it has some powerful medicine that will keep me from catching whatever it is that Jacinta has.'

'It certainly does,' Mrs Oliver replied. 'In fact, I've been testing it lately and every single person who has had it has kept the best of health. Wish I'd finished perfecting it before poor old Granny Bert almost caught her death. Now – Miss Jacinta, I think we should be putting you to bed. Up you go and I will be there shortly with some tea and toast. Alice-Miranda, can you get Jacinta organized with some books and a tray?' Mrs Oliver requested.

'Of course,' Alice-Miranda replied as she led Jacinta upstairs.

Chapter 15

With Jacinta tucked up in bed being fussed over by Mrs Oliver, Alice-Miranda headed off to the stables. She planned to take Bony out for a ride and find Lily, then Jasper and Lucas too.

'Hello, Max,' Alice-Miranda called as she entered the cool stone building which smelt of leather and wax and lucerne hay. Max was mucking out the stall her father's hunter, Shergar, usually occupied.

'Morning, miss, it's good to have you home,' he

replied. 'Bonaparte's in there.' He pointed to the stable at the end.

'Hello, fat boy,' she called. At the sound of her voice, Bonaparte whinnied in reply. Alice-Miranda opened the stable door and he immediately nuzzled her arm looking for treats. 'How about a ride?' she asked.

Max appeared beside her with the tack and the two of them began saddling and bridling the pony together.

'I lunged him this morning so he'll likely be a bit quiet,' Max explained. 'He's on a diet at the moment, and I've devised a strict exercise routine too. I've called it "Biggest loser for fat ponies with bad attitude",' Max laughed. Bonaparte turned around and bared his teeth. 'I reckon that pony is smarter than he looks.' Max bared his teeth back at Bony and began to struggle with the girth strap. Each time he pulled, Bonaparte took a deep breath and his stomach inflated.

'Come on, Bonaparte. Be a good boy and I'm sure I can find you some treats while we're out.' Alice-Miranda nuzzled his mane.

At the mention of treats Bonaparte whinnied and Max strained the girth strap to its usual notch.

Max gave Alice-Miranda a leg-up into the saddle. She checked her stirrups before urging Bonaparte out into the sunshine.

'Bye Max, see you later,' she called, then leaned forward and gave Bonaparte a scratch between the ears.

'Let's go and find Lily,' she said and gave his tummy a squeeze as they trotted down the drive.

It was a glorious morning. With the breeze on her face, Alice-Miranda clicked her tongue and Bonaparte lengthened his stride into a canter. She loved the rhythm of the horse under her – and although Bony was still considered a pony; just on fourteen hands – he was quite big enough to have a loping rather than bone-shuddering gait, especially for a child as small as she was.

'Hello, Mr Greening,' Alice-Miranda called as they neared the gatehouse. Bonaparte slowed to a trot then a lazy walk. Mr Greening was trimming a photinia hedge which had pushed its way through the fence and was poking untidily into the driveway.

He looked up and waved. 'Hello, there. You on your own?' he enquired.

'Yes, Jacinta's not feeling well so she's gone to bed. And just between you and me,' Alice-Miranda smiled, 'I think she's quite enjoying Mrs Oliver making a big fuss of her.'

Mr Greening laughed.

'So I thought it was a good opportunity to take Bony out – Jacinta's not fond of horses and I've been neglecting him since I arrived home. I'm off to see Lily,' Alice-Miranda babbled.

'Oh, I thought Lily would be up at the Hall with Mrs Greening and your mother and just about anyone else who knows anything about dusting and polishing and cleaning,' Mr Greening offered. 'I'm not going near the place this morning in case they put a bottle of silver polish in my hand.'

'No.' Alice-Miranda shook her head. 'Mummy said that Lily was busy with other things.'

'I'm surprised,' Mr Greening replied. 'I know it's all hands on deck so the place can be ready in time for Fri—' He stopped suddenly.

'Friday?' Alice-Miranda's eyes were wide. 'What's happening on Friday?'

'Oh, umm, nothing, nothing at all,' Mr Greening tried to backtrack.

'You're telling a big fat fib,' Alice-Miranda prodded. 'Last night Daddy said something and Mummy cut him off. I thought he said "par—". Is it a party? Let me see – why would we be having a party? It's not Mummy's birthday and it's not Daddy's or mine. I think Granny's is in a month or so. Oh!' Alice-Miranda's mouth formed a perfect letter 'o'. 'It's Aunt Charlotte's – it's her birthday on Saturday. Mummy and Daddy must be throwing a party for her. It must be a special one – I think she must be . . . now, let's see . . . I wonder how old she is? Daddy's forty-five and Mummy's forty and I know Aunt Charlotte is quite a lot younger than her . . .' Alice-Miranda thought for a moment. 'She must be turning thirty – that's it!'

Mr Greening frowned and looked as if he'd just been caught with his hand in Mrs Oliver's biscuit tin.

'That's it, isn't it?' Alice-Miranda exclaimed. 'There's a big party.' She was very pleased with herself for working it out.

'Well, I didn't tell you anything.' Mr Greening shook his head. 'And I will not confirm or deny – but don't you go saying anything to your mother or father.' He wagged his right forefinger at her. 'It's a surprise.'

'It's OK. I won't tell,' she promised. 'I'm very good at secrets. But what about a present?' Alice-Miranda thought out loud. 'I haven't got her anything and if I'm not supposed to know then I can hardly ask Mummy and Daddy to help me arrange one. Will you help me?' She beamed at Mr Greening. 'I think I've got an idea.'

'All right then – out with it.' Mr Greening put the hedge shears down and walked over to give Bonaparte a scratch on his head.

'Well, what do you think about . . .' Alice-Miranda lowered her voice – just in case the trees had ears.

Chapter 16

Mr Greening listened while Alice-Miranda explained exactly what she had in mind. 'Charlotte's always saying how much she misses Highton Hall. I'm sure that no one would notice if just one went missing. And I'm positive she'd have room for it.'

Mr Greening laughed and said that he would get straight to work. He didn't quite know how he would arrange things without arousing suspicion, but Alice-Miranda assured him that if anyone could get it done, he certainly could.

Bonaparte was dozing in the sunshine, occasionally twitching his ears or tail to get rid of a pesky fly.

'Well, I think we'll head over and see if Lily's home. But maybe we should call in and see Granny on the way.' Alice-Miranda pulled gently on the reins, and Bonaparte opened his eyes. 'I did promise we'd see her today. Come on, boy, let's go.' Alice-Miranda clicked her tongue and Bonaparte swayed lazily from side to side before walking forward. 'See you later, Mr Greening,' she winked. 'You're the best.'

'You take care there, lass.' He raised his hand to wave and winked back at her.

Alice-Miranda and Bonaparte trotted down the laneway towards Rose Cottage. She eased him into a canter again. Her mind was awhirl thinking about the surprise party on Friday.

Bonaparte slowed to a trot and then to a walk. Alice-Miranda pulled softly on the reins and he stopped outside the gate to Rose Cottage. She tied him carefully to the fence along the gravel road.

'You stay here, boy, and I'll be back soon. Maybe Granny has a carrot to spare,' she said, patting his neck. At the mention of food, his ears pricked up and he snickered. Alice-Miranda laughed. 'OK, I'll do my best,' she promised.

Alice-Miranda opened the creaky cottage gate and walked up the path. Just as she was about to enter the side door, something caught her eye. It was a black car, quite possibly the same one she and Jacinta had seen yesterday. It was parked around the back of the cottage, mostly hidden behind a screen of jasmine. Alice-Miranda headed straight into the kitchen as she had done a hundred times before, wondering if she might meet the car's owner.

'Hello Granny, it's Alice-Miranda.' She waited for a reply but none came. 'Hello, is anyone home?' she said again.

Upstairs the floorboards creaked.

'Granny, are you up there?' Alice-Miranda called. There was no reply and the noise from upstairs stopped. She headed into the hallway towards the stairs when she spotted Granny in the front sitting room, dozing in her favourite armchair with a steaming cup of tea on the table beside her.

'Granny, Granny,' she whispered, not wanting to startle her.

Alice-Miranda thought it was funny that Granny should make herself a cup of tea and then doze off before drinking it, but she *had* been unwell and was getting old. Granny's breathing was deep and even.

There was a loud grunt and Alice-Miranda watched, hopeful that she might open her eyes.

She didn't, and Alice-Miranda retreated to the kitchen. She couldn't help wondering who owned that car and where they might be. She knew that Daisy was up at the Hall with her mother and the rest of the cleaning team. Alice-Miranda had an uneasy feeling that she and Granny were not alone. And there was only one way to find out.

Rose Cottage wasn't quite as small as the name implied. There was a large eat-in kitchen with its own side porch. On the opposite side of the long hallway was a pretty sitting room, then further along the hall were the stairs and beyond those, a funny sort of a utility room which Daisy used as a laundry and storage area. It had a door which led straight out to the back garden. Upstairs there were three large bedrooms and a bathroom.

'Is anyone up here?' Alice-Miranda called as she bounded up the stairs straight into Granny's pink bedroom, which smelt of lavender oil and starched sheets. There was no one there. She wandered into the matching pink bathroom, with its 1940s suite which still sparkled like new. Alice-Miranda was admiring Daisy's housekeeping skills when something caught her eye. She could have sworn she saw something move in the mirror behind her.

'Is anyone there?' She scampered to the landing. From Daisy's bedroom at the end of the hall she heard a scratching noise. 'Hello,' she called. It seemed to be coming from inside the wardrobe.

Alice-Miranda strode into the room and wrenched open the cedar door.

'Mr Pippin, what on earth are you doing in here? You poor man – you must be famished. Come on out of there.' Alice-Miranda reached into the cupboard and gathered Mr Pippin into her arms. He began to purr loudly.

Downstairs a door slammed.

'Granny,' she called. 'Are you all right?'

Alice-Miranda immediately put Mr Pippin down on Daisy's bed and headed for the stairs. A snore from the front room told her that Granny was still fast asleep.

Alice-Miranda bounded down the stairs to the utility room. She wrenched open the back door and poked her head outside. The black car was still there, but there was no sign of anyone. She was about to take a proper look around when the sound of Bonaparte whinnying with great gusto convinced her otherwise.

'OK, OK, I'm coming,' she called and retreated to the kitchen where she began to rummage through the refrigerator looking for a carrot. In the crisper she found half a cabbage, some potatoes, a few brussels sprouts and finally several carrots. As she reached in for one she noticed something else in the bottom of the drawer. It looked like a folded newspaper, but when she took it out she realized that it was a rather yellowed set of drawings. She placed the tattered documents and a large carrot on the kitchen table before closing the fridge door.

Alice-Miranda opened the drawings and realized they were plans. Looking at their colour and condition she thought they were quite likely the original drawings of Rose Cottage and the gatehouse. There was a plan of the stables as well.

'What a curious place to keep these,' she said to herself. Alice-Miranda thought that she must tell Daisy about what she had found – and ask her about the car and its owner too.

Granny Bert was still snoring loudly. Alice-Miranda folded the plans and laid them in the middle of the table. 'I'll come back later, Granny,' she whispered before heading out through the kitchen door.

'Bony, look what I've found,' Alice-Miranda called, waving the carrot in the air. She was surprised when he did not reply. 'Bonaparte, I've got you a fat carrot.'

Alice-Miranda rounded the path to find that Bonaparte was gone. She ran to the gate, expecting that he had somehow managed to get loose and that she would find him grazing along the side of the lane, but he was nowhere to be seen.

'Bonaparte!' she called. 'Bony!' Alice-Miranda scampered down to the sheds to see if he had got into the feed. He wasn't there. She darted to the other side of Rose Cottage where lush grass grew along the edge of the fence. 'Oh no! The cabbages!' She clutched her hands to her face.

Alice-Miranda raced as quickly as she could to Mr Greening's prized vegetable patch. It was hidden further along the path behind the machinery shed. The gate was open and there, in the middle of the cabbages, Bonaparte was chomping at pace.

'You naughty boy!' She charged into the patch and snatched up the reins. 'How did you get in here?' Alice-Miranda tugged hard, trying to lift his head but a determined pony is no match for a slight girl of seven and a half. 'Bonaparte,' she gasped. 'Come on!'

From the corner of her eye Alice-Miranda noticed a figure. She looked up to see Lucas straddling the fence.

'Hello Lucas, thank goodness you're here. Could you help me with Bonaparte please?' she asked.

'Why?' he glared. 'He's your pony.'

'Yes, but he's very strong, especially when he's eating cabbages. I'd be very grateful if you could come and help me,' she tried again.

'No,' he replied.

'I can't imagine how he got in here – look at the size of that new bolt,' Alice-Miranda puffed.

'Don't look at me,' Lucas sneered.

'Lucas, *please* can you help me?' Alice-Miranda begged.

He swung his leg over and sat on top of the rail. 'I'd rather just watch. Why don't you call your boyfriend? I'm sure little Jas would love to rescue you.'

'Lucas, Jasper is not my boyfriend. I'd really appreciate it if you would stop teasing. Anyway, I don't know where he is and after what happened earlier I think he's quite upset with me,' Alice-Miranda began.

'Why would I stop teasing you? You're a stuck-up little princess who lives in a castle,' Lucas snarled.

'Lucas, with all respect you don't even know me. And I'm not a princess and we don't live in a castle at all. Mummy and Daddy's friend Lord Gisborne lives in a castle – not a very big one but it does have a moat and Aunty Gee, well she has several palaces and they even have dungeons and armour and that sort of thing, but we live in a Hall and there is a big difference,' Alice-Miranda chattered.

She tugged at Bonaparte's bridle and managed to get him to lift his head ever so slightly before he plunged it back into the middle of a half-chewed cabbage.

'Listen to you,' Lucas sneered. '*I'm not a princess and we don't live in a castle – it's a Hall,*' he mocked her. 'You don't even know how spoilt you are. You make me sick.' He leaped from the top rail and hit the ground outside the fence. 'I'd help you if I could be bothered – but I can't!' he spat before stalking off around the corner of the shed.

Alice-Miranda let him go. For now she had to get Bonaparte out of the cabbages or he could be in real trouble – his feast would almost surely give him colic and Mr Greening would be cross about the mess he'd made.

'Do you need zum help zere Alice-Miranda?' a thickly accented voice called from the back of the machinery shed. It was Heinrich, Jasper and Poppy's father.

'Oh Heinrich, yes, thank you. He's such a little monster and I just can't lift his head,' she said, still tugging ferociously.

Heinrich marched into the patch and jerked Bonaparte's head upwards. Bonaparte's ears flattened and he snorted. With a tight grip on the reins, Heinrich led him out of the garden with Alice-Miranda following a safe distance from his hind legs.

'One zing's for sure' – Heinrich handed the reins to Alice-Miranda as he closed the gate and secured the latch – 'Someone left zat gate open – even Houdini horse here could not have opened it himself.'

'Oh.' Alice-Miranda contemplated this. 'I *thought* I had tied him up pretty well at Granny Bert's too.'

'Vell, you best take him home and I will call Max to get Dr Vanner. You know zat pony just has to look at a cabbage and he gets ze colic,' Heinrich warned. 'Alzough last time he got in zere, vhile you vere at school, he just got very bad vind,' he laughed.

'Thank you, Heinrich.' Alice-Miranda smiled as she began to lead Bonaparte down the path to

133

the lane. She turned back, 'Heinrich, Lucas was here before.'

Heinrich shook his head. 'Zat boy is none of your concern, miss. Zum zings are best left alone.'

'I'm worried about him,' Alice-Miranda said gently. 'And I'd really like to be his friend – if he'd let me.'

'You're a good girl, Alice-Miranda. For your own sake, stay away from him for ze moment. He's got a lot on his mind for a young boy. But vun day, I'm sure he'll come right,' Heinrich advised.

This time she did not argue.

Alice-Miranda led Bonaparte past the machinery shed and Rose Cottage. Her thoughts were racing – she was thinking about Granny, worrying about Bony and wondering who on earth owned that car.

They walked quickly back along the laneway and into the drive. Mr Greening had disappeared – she would find him and apologise for Bonaparte's bad behaviour later. She led the pony up the long driveway and around to the stables where Max was waiting.

'I can't believe he's done it again.' He shook his head. 'Dr Wanner is on his way, I'll keep walking fat boy until he gets here.'

'I can do that,' Alice-Miranda offered. 'It's my fault he got into the patch, I should have tied him up more firmly.'

'It's all right, miss. I'll take him.' Max took the reins.

'At least let me help you get his saddle off. I can give him a bit of a rub – hopefully push some of that wind through.' Alice-Miranda patted Bony's shoulder as she spoke. 'He can't have been in there for very long. I was only inside with Granny for ten minutes at most. She was sound asleep.'

'Last time he ate half the vegetable patch, so it sounds like we might get off a bit easier this time – although I'm still not looking forward to the air in here tonight.' Max rolled his eyes. 'You know, I gave him a new name when it happened before – Bonafarte.' Max laughed at his own joke.

Alice-Miranda giggled. 'My friend Millie would have loved that,' she replied.

Max led the swelling beast into the stables and eased his bridle off, putting his halter and lead rope on. Bony stood relatively still, although when he began lifting his back leg and trying to kick at his stomach, it was clear that his feast was starting to have an ill effect. Alice-Miranda undid the girth strap and Max lifted the saddle off and placed it in the tack room. He retrieved a brush and handed it to Alice-Miranda who began stroking Bonaparte's neck. When she reached his back he started to flinch and when she touched his stomach he snapped at her head, grabbing a few strands of curly hair.

'Ow,' Alice-Miranda squealed. 'It's not my fault you have a tummy ache, you greedy guts.'

'Best stay away from his belly,' Max advised. 'It's all right, here's Dr Wanner now.

'Morning all.' Dr Wanner gathered his black bag from the front seat of the Landcruiser and strode into the stables. 'Now, Bonaparte,' he addressed the horse. 'What have you been up to this time?'

He examined Bonaparte thoroughly and got a nip and a kick for his trouble.

'I think he'll be fine – just keep a close eye on him and don't let him lie down,' Dr Wanner concluded as he gently stroked Bonaparte's nose. 'But you must keep him away from the vegetables, Alice-Miranda. He just can't help himself and I'd hate to see anything happen to the little beast.'

Bonaparte bared his teeth in reply.

'Thank you, Dr Wanner,' Alice-Miranda smiled. 'Somehow I don't think this was all his own doing.'

'No, someone must have left the gate open – I saw the size of that bolt Mr Greening installed after the last incident when I was checking on one of the cows the other week. Anyway, must be off – the Rector's hens have stopped laying and he's complaining that he hasn't had a decent breakfast in weeks.' Dr Wanner gathered his bag and headed back to the car.

'I'll stay with him now,' said Max as he rubbed Bony's ears.

'Well, if you're sure. I might go and see how Jacinta is getting on and then I will have to find Mr Greening and apologize for Bony's path of destruction.' Alice-Miranda walked around and blew gently into Bonaparte's nose. He nuzzled her back. 'Now, you be a good boy and stay out of trouble,' she whispered, 'even though I don't think this is *all* your fault.'

Her earlier encounter with Lucas had given her a very uneasy feeling and although she didn't like to, she couldn't help but wonder if he might have had something to do with Bony's unscheduled visit to the vegetable patch.

Chapter 17

Alice-Miranda now had lots of things to do. First she wanted to check on Jacinta, then apologise to Mr Greening, talk to Daisy – and Lily too if she could find her – make up with Jasper and see Lucas. Later, when her father and Mr Ridley returned, she planned to ask Mr Ridley about the real reason he was here. And then there was that black car and its mysterious owner. It was wonderful to be home from school but she couldn't believe how busy she was – there was certainly no time to relax.

She bounded off to see Jacinta.

'Hello.' Jacinta looked up from her book, then sneezed loudly.

'Bless you,' Alice-Miranda replied. 'Are you feeling any better?'

'No, I'm worse.' Jacinta sniffled into a tissue. 'But I can't complain about the food.' She nodded towards the tea tray on the table beside the bed. It was laden with egg sandwiches, honey crumpets and a large piece of chocolate cake. 'Trouble is, I don't feel much like eating. I hope Mrs Oliver won't be upset.'

'Of course not,' Alice-Miranda replied as she picked up a sandwich and began to nibble.

'What have you been doing?' Jacinta asked.

'Well, I took Bonaparte for a ride and we saw Mr Greening and then I went to find Lily but I decided I should visit Granny Bert first but she was asleep and then Bony got into the vegetable patch and he was being such a brute and then Lucas wouldn't help me but luckily Heinrich did, so I walked Bony home and Dr Wanner's just been to see him to make sure he doesn't get colic. Oh, and I saw a big black car parked around the back of Rose Cottage – I think it might have been the same one that nearly ran us over in the lane yesterday.' Alice-Miranda finally ran out of steam.

'Who does it belong to?' Jacinta demanded.

'I don't know.' Alice-Miranda kicked off her boots and climbed onto the bed, tucking her knees underneath her. 'I was on my way to see Granny when I spotted it. When I went inside she was sitting in the front room dozing. It was a little odd: she had a steaming cup of tea beside her and she was fast asleep,' Alice-Miranda mused. 'And I thought I heard footsteps on the upstairs landing so I went up to take a look around.'

Jacinta's eyes widened. 'Was someone in the house? Perhaps they were upstairs snooping about and they made Granny Bert a cup of tea with something in it to put her to sleep.'

'I don't think so,' Alice-Miranda grinned. 'I'm sure there was no one there,' she said firmly, trying to convince herself. But the creaking floorboards and slamming door didn't do anything to support her argument. 'I'm sure it was just the old house grumbling and groaning. If you lie here in the quiet for long enough, the Hall will start talking to you too. Oh, and Mr Pippin was locked in Daisy's wardrobe.'

'Who's Mr Pippin?' Jacinta sat forward.

'Daisy's funny old dribbly cat,' Alice-Miranda replied. 'Anyway, I don't think Granny and Daisy have anything anyone would want to snoop around for.'

As those words slipped from her mouth, Alice-Miranda remembered the plans. She had assumed that Granny had put them in the crisper by mistake, but now she wasn't so sure. And she had put them out on the kitchen table for anyone to see. All at once, she had a very bad feeling.

'You should go back and see what you can find,' Jacinta urged. 'I'd love to come but Mrs Oliver has called the doctor to see me – in case it's the flu or something. I hate being sick,' she said with a cough. 'It's so unfair to miss all the fun.'

'OK. I'll head over and check on Granny again now.' Alice-Miranda was a little relieved to have an excuse to go and ask about the plans. 'Just in case you're right, which I'm sure you're not. Who'd want to hurt Granny? And besides, I think she's very capable of looking after herself.'

'She'd send thieves running for cover just to get away from all that whining.' Jacinta giggled, which dissolved into a cough like the bark of a seal.

Alice-Miranda slid off the side of the bed. 'Can I get you anything?' she asked.

'Glass of water,' Jacinta wheezed. Her nose was getting redder by the minute. She took a sip. 'Just go and find out who owns that black car.' Jacinta managed a half smile before burrowing down into the mountain of pillows behind her. 'And then come back and tell me all about it.'

Chapter 18

Alice-Miranda charged off into the garden, heading for Rose Cottage.

It was quite a long walk but her legs carried her swiftly through the meadow. All the while she kept an eye out for Jasper and Poppy, and Lucas. Scampering over the stile, she ran down the laneway towards Rose Cottage. There was no sign of the black car.

'Granny, are you there?' she called as she clattered through the side door and into the kitchen.

'Of course I'm here.' Granny Bert was sitting in the very same place she had been before. 'I've been trying to have a nap but with all that noise, I fear I'll never get any rest,' she grumbled.

'But I came a while ago and you were sound asleep. Right here.' Alice-Miranda plonked onto the armchair beside her.

'I don't know what you're talking about, young lady. I have been wide awake all morning. I've not even had a cup of tea, with Daisy up there at the Hall helping your mother.'

Alice-Miranda looked over to the table where she had seen the cup of tea with her own eyes. It was gone. She ran to the kitchen. The cup was nowhere to be seen. And the plans were missing too.

'I must be losing my mind,' Alice-Miranda sighed.

'Do you think you could put the pot on, young lady?' Granny called.

Alice-Miranda was lost in her thoughts. She replayed the events of her previous visit. There *was* a cup of tea on that side table and Granny *was* asleep and she most certainly had left those plans in the middle of the kitchen table.

'Did you hear me?' Granny called again.

Alice-Miranda looked up. 'Sorry, what did you say?'

'Are you deaf, dear?' Granny growled. 'I asked if you could possibly make me a cup of tea. I'm rather parched and I wouldn't mind some of that lovely lemon cake too if there's any left.'

'Of course.' Alice-Miranda pulled the footstool over to the kitchen sink and began to fill the kettle. She touched the side of the metal vessel – it was still just slightly warm. She wasn't going mad at all. Someone had been in the house earlier and she was determined to find out who it was and what they were doing there.

Alice-Miranda made Granny her tea and cut a very large slice of lemon cake. Although Granny protested loudly that she would never eat that much in a month, she managed to plough through it all and asked if there might be a couple of biscuits she could have by her side – just in case Daisy was late getting home. Alice-Miranda asked Granny if she had had any visitors that morning.

'Visitors, I haven't had any visitors since you were here yesterday,' Granny pouted. 'It's been a lonely time for an old woman with not even her closest neighbours to call on her. Everyone's so jolly busy.'

'But Granny, I've seen a black car here a couple of times now. Who does it belong to?' Alice-Miranda asked.

'Oh, just a friend,' she replied. 'Lovely man. I've been helping him with something – for your parents.' Granny's lips drew together as though she was sucking on a very sour lemon.

'Was he here this morning?' Alice-Miranda reached out and placed her tiny hand on Granny's. Her skin was like tissue paper.

'Of course not. I told you before that I haven't had any visitors since you were here last time. Do you think I'm losing my marbles, young lady?' Granny grouched.

'Of course not,' Alice-Miranda replied. 'It's just that I saw that car when I was here earlier this morning.'

'But you weren't here earlier this morning. You mustn't tell tales to make yourself feel better. I know you've got more interesting things to do than sit here with me.'

'But Granny, I promise I was here earlier,' Alice-Miranda protested.

'Alice-Miranda, if you were here I would have remembered. I think it's time for you to go home.'

Granny withdrew her hand and folded her arms in front of her.

There was no point arguing. Alice-Miranda picked up the teacup and saucer and set them down on the sink. She walked back into the sitting room and reached up to give Granny a peck on her powdered cheek.

'Goodbye, Granny,' she smiled. 'I'll come and see you again soon, I promise.'

'Goodbye, dear.' Granny stared vacantly at the window. 'And I'd rather you didn't make promises you can't keep.'

Chapter 19

Alice-Miranda's mind was racing. *If I'm not going mad*, she thought to herself, *then I think someone must have put something in Granny's tea*. She wondered what sort of medicine made people go to sleep and forget things.

Something else was bothering Alice-Miranda. She needed to find Jasper. She felt awful about what had happened earlier and wanted to make sure that he was all right.

Alice-Miranda left Rose Cottage and ran down

the lane to Jasper's house, where she knocked loudly on the back door. Heinrich was in the kitchen having lunch.

'Hello Alice-Miranda,' he called. 'Come in, come in. How is zat pony of yours?'

'He's fine,' she replied. 'I don't think he actually ate that much. Is Lily home?' It had just occurred to her that she might have a chance to talk to her before seeing Jasper. Hopefully she could clear up one of the mysteries.

'No. She's gone to ze town today.' Heinrich shook his head. 'Won't be back until late.'

'Is Jasper in?'

'He's upstairs – in a bit of a mood, I zink. Poppy's gone to play wiz a little friend in ze village. I 'ave to pick her up later. Better not forget or I'll be in trouble wiz her mother.' He winked. 'Why don't you go up and see Jas – might make 'im feel better.'

Alice-Miranda bounded upstairs, eager to put things right with her friend. He was in the room under the eaves, playing with his models.

'Hello Jasper,' she said from the doorway. 'I've come to apologise.'

'For what?' He didn't look up.

'You know – for before . . . with Lucas. I didn't mean for him to wreck your model. I was only trying to help,' Alice-Miranda explained.

Jasper stood up and walked around to the other side of the table. He picked up two soldiers and moved them to another part of the battlefield.

'I'm sorry,' Alice-Miranda tried again. 'I was hoping we could spend some time together. Jacinta's not feeling well so she's gone to bed and Bonaparte's in trouble,' she began. 'I've really missed you.'

Jasper brushed a hand across his eye. 'Why did you have to go away to that stupid school?' He looked up at her.

'But I love school,' Alice-Miranda replied, 'and I'll be home every couple of months.'

'It's not the same,' said Jasper. 'And now that he's here, he's wrecked everything.'

'Who?' Alice-Miranda asked.

'Who do you think?' Jasper stood up and faced her.

'Oh,' Alice-Miranda whispered.

Jasper looked as though he might cry.

'Why is he here, Jasper?' she asked.

He didn't reply.

'Do you want to go for a walk?' Alice-Miranda suggested. Jasper nodded his head ever so slightly. 'Come on then.'

She walked downstairs with Jasper two steps behind her.

'Bye kids – go and have zum fun now,' Heinrich said as the children walked through the kitchen.

'Goodbye Heinrich,' Alice-Miranda called. Jasper raised his hand to wave at his father.

Chapter 20

Alice-Miranda and Jasper headed off into the long meadow towards the stream. Before Alice-Miranda had left for school, she and Jasper – with lots of direction from Poppy – had built a hidden cubby beneath the branches of an enormous fir tree. For weeks they had spent every afternoon there.

The towering trunk soared into the sky and the branches had grown so long and heavy that they hung down to the ground to form a natural shelter. Once the children were inside no one would ever have known they were there.

Alice-Miranda lifted the branch that guarded the entrance. The cubby was cavernous and it was just as she had left it – even the teacups and saucers were still sitting on the table.

Jasper finally spoke. 'We haven't been here at all since you left.'

'Why not?' Alice-Miranda asked as she poked around examining the various bits and pieces.

'Because it wasn't the same without you. I told Poppy that it had been taken over by witches so she wouldn't want to come any more,' he explained.

'Poor Poppy – she's terrified of witches. I'll have to tell her that they've moved out. This place needs a bit of a tidy up.' She set forth stacking the china plates and emptying the grungy water from the teacups. Alice-Miranda found an old straw broom and began sweeping the dead pine needles into a pile in one corner. She moved the gaudy green armchairs to face each other and picked up a battered accordion from the ground. It wheezed a very flat C as she placed it on the pine dresser.

When the children decided to make the cubby, Alice-Miranda had asked her father and mother if she could have some furniture for it. Her father suggested they could have some especially made but Alice-Miranda thought that was too silly for words. She loved her father very much but she thought he was a little bit prone to spoiling her. Instead she remembered that there were a whole lot of old bits and pieces in one of the sheds near Rose Cottage that would be perfect. So Mr Greening had helped the children transport two armchairs and a pine dresser, an old kitchen cabinet with a sink, a pine table with four chairs, a mirror and a tarnished brass light fitting, which they suspended from a branch inside. Heinrich had found a moth-eaten accordion to add to their treasures.

'So, can you tell me about Lucas?' Alice-Miranda asked as she stacked the plates into the dresser.

'He's our cousin,' Jasper said.

'Yes, I know that. But why is he staying here?'

'His mother has gone away. He was supposed to be at boarding school but that didn't work out so my mother offered to let him stay with us until Aunty Kitty comes back,' he explained.

'So Aunty Kitty is your *mother's* sister?' Alice-Miranda asked. She plonked onto one of the armchairs. Jasper sat down opposite.

'Yes. But I've never even met her. Dad says she's the black sheep of the family – whatever that means.'

'I think it's like the odd one out. The one that doesn't quite fit in,' Alice-Miranda explained. 'Where's Lucas's father?'

'I don't know. Nobody talks about him.'

'Oh.' Alice-Miranda twisted a stray curl around her finger and examined the ends. 'Do you know where your aunt has gone?' she questioned.

'To America, I think. She's a costume designer for movies. Mum said that she couldn't take Lucas with her because she has to move around a lot. That's why she sent him to boarding school. Anyway, Lucas has been horrid ever since he arrived. He hates everything and I hate him,' Jasper spat.

Alice-Miranda frowned. Jasper was the kindest, most thoughtful boy she had ever known. He never said bad things about anyone and she'd certainly never heard him say that he hated anyone before. She needed to talk to Lucas at once.

Alice-Miranda stood up. 'Jasper, it can't be as bad as all that. Lucas must be terribly lonely. I'm sure I would feel very sad and scared if I'd been sent to live with cousins I'd never even met before,' she soothed.

Jasper couldn't imagine Alice-Miranda ever feeling lonely. She made friends with everyone.

'Well, I wouldn't steal their things and break stuff and tease them all the time,' Jasper replied.

'Of course not.' She walked towards the door, then stopped and turned to her friend. 'I've only been home one day and so far I have had stones thrown at me, almost been run over by a big black car, my pony has made a mess of the vegetable patch, I've had a row with you, and Granny Bert thinks I tell lies. I'd rather like to start my holidays again, if I can?'

Alice-Miranda promptly walked out of the cubby, turned around and knocked on a branch as loudly as she could – which wasn't very loud, so she yelled 'knock knock'. When she re-entered she walked over to Jasper and held out her hand.

'Hello, my name is Alice-Miranda Highton-Smith-Kennington-Jones and I'm very pleased to be home.'

Jasper stood up and reached his hand out to meet Alice-Miranda's. 'And I'm Jasper Bauer and it's really good to see you.' The two friends laughed as they shook hands.

Jasper asked Alice-Miranda about school and Alice-Miranda told him all about Miss Grimm and Alethea and all of the challenges she'd had to complete. For a little while she forgot about Mr

Ridley and the mystery of the black car. They chatted for ages about this and that until Alice-Miranda's stomach rumbled so loudly Jasper thought it was a wild animal outside. They decided to head back to the Hall for a sandwich.

'What did you say before – about almost being run over?' Jasper asked as they walked through into the walled garden.

Alice-Miranda explained about the black sedan at the back of Rose Cottage. She told Jasper about her visit to Granny and the cup of tea and Granny's lost memory.

'I've seen that car,' Jasper told her, 'and I met the man who drives it.'

Alice-Miranda's eyes widened. 'Who is he?'

'I don't know. He was poking around in the machinery shed and when I asked what he was doing he said that he was meeting a man about a tractor. I didn't think that was very likely seeing that my dad handles all the business about the machinery. And besides, who wears a suit to go and look at a tractor? When I said I would go and find Dad, he disappeared.'

'That does seem strange,' Alice-Miranda agreed. It appeared that Jacinta was right after all.

Chapter 21

The next few days seemed to disappear in a blink. Alice-Miranda still hadn't managed to talk to Lily – who could apparently make herself invisible at will. Mr Ridley was equally difficult to pin down. When he and her father had returned from their long ride on Monday afternoon, Mr Ridley vanished and was nowhere to be seen at all the next day. Her mother said that he had some important things to attend to and there would be plenty of time to get to know him later in the week. But then mid-week he was called back into town on urgent business, so he packed his bag and up and away he flew with Cyril and Birdy. He had said he hoped to be back before the weekend but there was still no sign of him.

Dr Marsh declared that Jacinta had a nasty bout of flu. Although she was getting stronger every day, she'd promised the doctor she'd take a few days' bed rest. So Alice-Miranda spent most of the time romping about with Poppy and Jasper just as she had always done. They all kept an eye out for the black car and its mysterious driver but there was no sign of either of them. Lucas seemed to have found a cloak of invisibility too – despite visiting Jasper and Poppy's house, Alice-Miranda never caught as much as a glimpse of him.

Granny Bert was well on the mend, grumbling and grizzling as good as new. Alice-Miranda decided not to ask her anything more about that strange morning with the tea and the car. There was no point upsetting her again. She decided to talk to Daisy instead.

On Wednesday morning Alice-Miranda was on her way to meet Jasper when she spied Daisy trimming the roses near the fence.

'Hello Daisy,' she called. 'Have you got a minute?'

Daisy looked up and smiled. 'Hello darling girl. How can I help you?'

'Well, there's been something bothering me quite a bit and I thought you might be able to help. I really don't want to worry anyone at home. They're all so busy getting ready for the weekend, which – I know – I'm not supposed to know about. Anyway, it's probably best I talk to you. It's about Granny.'

Daisy snipped another bloom.

'When you were helping Mummy at the Hall the other morning I called in to see Granny and she was asleep,' Alice-Miranda began.

'Oh, that's not unusual and since she's been sick she's been sleeping all the time,' Daisy replied.

'It's just that there was a black car parked around the back of the cottage and when I came into the house there was a noise upstairs and then I called Granny and she was sound asleep in the front room. The odd thing is, there was a steaming cup of tea beside her.'

'Oh, perhaps she managed to shuffle out to the kitchen to make it.' Daisy cut a ragged looking flower.

'Well, the tea was really hot and Granny was fast asleep. It seemed odd to me. I hope you don't mind but I took a look around upstairs – I had the strangest feeling that there was someone else in the house. Anyway, there was no one there – except poor old Mr Pippin locked in your wardrobe. And then I heard a door slam downstairs. I looked out the back but there was no one there. Oh, except there was a big black car. Anyway, I decided to leave Granny and come back later but that's when Bony got into the vegetable patch. When I did come back the teacup was gone and Granny was very cross with me for not visiting her earlier. I asked her about the owner of the black car and she said that it belonged to a friend who was doing something for Mummy and Daddy.'

Daisy absently lopped the head of a full bloom, sending it tumbling to the ground. A trickle of blood ran down her arm.

'Daisy, you're bleeding!' Alice-Miranda exclaimed.

'Oh.' Daisy dropped the cuttings. 'It's only a thorn. I can assure you there's nothing to worry about, Alice-Miranda. Granny's just getting old and forgetting things. She probably put the teacup away herself. And the wind must have caught the back door – it has a terrible habit of flying open on its own. I'm sure there's nothing more to it than that.'

Alice-Miranda rummaged around in her pocket and found a tissue, which she handed to Daisy.

'But who owns the black car?' Alice-Miranda insisted.

'No one important.' Daisy shook her head. Alice-Miranda was not convinced. 'Look there's Jasper,' said Daisy, pointing. 'Why don't you run along and play.'

'But there was something else too,' Alice-Miranda began.

'Sorry, sweetheart, I have to go. Granny has a doctor's appointment in the village and we daren't be late.'

Daisy rushed off before Alice-Miranda had time to mention anything about the plans.

Chapter 22

On Thursday afternoon Jacinta felt well enough to go for a walk in the garden. She thought she might find Alice-Miranda and the others and although she loved being the centre of Mrs Oliver's attention, she was feeling much better and had started worrying that she hadn't done any training since the weekend. There was nothing she wanted more than to win a medal at the junior Olympics and she knew it wouldn't happen if she lay about in bed eating cakes and drinking tea.

'Where do you think I might find Alice-Miranda and Jasper?' Jacinta asked when Mrs Oliver came to collect her tea tray.

'Well, I heard Alice-Miranda telling her mother that she was meeting Jasper and Poppy at the cubby. It's a bit of a walk though, dear – would you like me to have Mr Greening drop you down there?'

'If it's all right with you, I'd really love to go for a walk – if you could just tell me how to find it, I'm sure I can make it on my own.'

Mrs Oliver gently laid the back of her hand on Jacinta's forehead. She then put each of her palms on Jacinta's cheeks and nodded her head.

'Temperature seems to be gone – and I must admit you have been the model patient, my dear. I think a walk might be just the tonic,' Mrs Oliver replied. She opened the top drawer of the cedar tallboy, retrieving a pair of socks and a pink checked shirt. She opened the wardrobe and found some jeans.

'Why don't you get dressed while I take the tea tray downstairs? When you're ready, come and see me in the kitchen and I can draw you a map of how to find the cubby.' She smiled at Jacinta. Dolly had grown rather fond of her little patient over the week – perhaps all the more so because the latest edition of *Women's Daily* contained a whole page about Jacinta's mother and her latest outing in Rome. Dolly had shown the article to Shilly and shaken her head. Ambrosia Headlington-Bear had not called once to enquire after Jacinta's wellbeing – even after Cecelia had alerted her to the fact that she was rather unwell.

'Not a mother's bootlace,' Mrs Oliver had muttered under her breath before taking Jacinta an extra piece of devil's food cake that afternoon.

Jacinta got dressed as instructed, grabbed her pink jacket and headed to the kitchen.

'Oh, I was just about to pop up and remind you about taking a jacket, Jacinta. It's warm outside now but once the sun dips it gets chilly. Good girl. I've drawn you a map – it's a bit scratchy but you should be able to find your way. And just in case you get lost, take the spare phone. I've programmed the house number into the speed dial, so just give a ring and one of us will be down to find you.'

Jacinta spent a few minutes going over the map with Mrs Oliver, who then handed her a small rucksack with some apples and four pieces of hummingbird cake – just in case anyone was hungry.

She set off across the driveway, through the walled garden and into the long meadow. She practically bounced – happy to be outside again on what was a most sparkling day. She could see the giant fir tree along the creek line where she expected to find her friends.

Jacinta turned and walked backwards, taking in the view of Highton Hall, when rather abruptly she was on her back, legs in the air, kicking like a stranded tortoise.

'Ow, why don't you watch where you're going!' a voice growled.

Jacinta rolled over to face her attacker.

'Me!' She scrambled to her feet. 'Why are you lying there in the grass in the first place? Of course I didn't see you.' And then she realized who she was talking to. 'You! I see your manners haven't improved in the past few days.' Jacinta narrowed her eyes.

'And you're still the same stuck-up spoilt rich brat too. Good to know some things don't change,' he spat back at her.

'What are you doing here anyway?' Jacinta looked around and realized that from this position he was completely hidden but had a very clear view of the fir tree. 'Are you spying on them?' she demanded.

'Why would I do that? I couldn't care less about them. I was just minding my own business,' he retaliated.

'And what exactly *is* your business, Lucassss?' Jacinta hissed his name.

'That's none of *your* business either,' he replied.

'Really! Well, I'm sure Alice-Miranda and Jasper will have something to say about that – and your Aunt Lily too.' Her shoulders rose and she exhaled loudly.

Lucas said nothing. He stood up and met her gaze, but this time she noticed something different in his eyes. Something Jacinta had seen before, in her own reflection.

'Go ahead and tell on me then. It won't make any difference. I'm sure that they're sending me away next week. I'm way too much trouble,' he said, his voice dripping with sarcasm.

'Where are you going?' Jacinta asked, softening just a little.

'Back to boarding school, I suppose. Where my mother left me. Lily's been to see them and patch things up. Probably asked your little friend's father and mother to make a donation or something so they could "overlook my issues".'

'What issues?' Jacinta asked.

Lucas kicked at the ground. 'Let's just say that I picked a fight with the wrong kid.'

'What do you mean?' Jacinta wasn't about to give up any time soon. 'What did you do?'

'I punched him in the nose.'

'What for?' Jacinta continued.

'Lots of things. The guy's a twit. He started picking on this other little kid from the minute he arrived. Told him he had to do everything he said and if he didn't, well, the kid copped it.'

Jacinta raised her eyebrows. 'How?'

'Honey in his bed sheets and mashed cockroaches in his toothbrush, for starters,' Lucas replied.

'That's terrible!' Jacinta exclaimed. 'Did anyone tell the teachers?'

'They tried, but no one would listen. This kid has everyone fooled.'

'It sounds like the bully at our school. She was asked to leave last term because the headmistress finally realized she was a horror. They're probably related,' Jacinta smiled. 'So it's true then, that you were expelled?'

'Yeah, that's why I'm here, having so much fun,' Lucas sneered.

'You know, it's not true what you said before about Hugh and Cecelia,' Jacinta began. 'I know they wouldn't pay off a school like that. They're not that sort of people.'

'Yeah right. Rich people are all the same in my books. Only want you around if you're perfect and well behaved and have good manners and stuff. Or else they can pay to get rid of you.'

'That's certainly not true. I'm not perfect and sometimes I have the worst manners ever. In fact, I'm known as my school's second best tantrum thrower.'

'You. Are you kidding me? What have you ever done?' Lucas stared.

'Well, let's just see. I hated school so much last year that I stole the school flag and hung it from my bedroom window, and I ordered a huge box of liquorice which I ate every night after 5 p.m.. I thought they'd have to send me home for sure. It's one of our school rules, you know.'

'What? Not stealing flags?' Lucas scoffed.

'No, not eating liquorice after 5 p.m.,' Jacinta retorted.

'And did they?' Lucas asked.

'Did they what?'

'Send you home, of course,' he demanded.

'No. They didn't. They rang my parents and asked them to come and get me but Mummy was too busy with her friends and Daddy was away on business. So instead I had detention for a month.'

'But weren't your parents angry?' Lucas pulled at a long stem of grass.

'Yes, of course they were. Mummy was furious because she had to take a very long phone call from Miss Reedy and it interrupted her manicure.'

'My mother wasn't very happy about what happened with me either.'

'What about your father?' Jacinta asked. 'Where's he?'

'I don't even know who he is. And I don't want to talk about it. It's none of your business,' Lucas snapped. 'Anyway, is that all you've done?'

'Well, no. I cried like a baby every night for a month. Homesickness is punishable by expulsion, you know.'

'Really?' Lucas looked moderately impressed. 'Have you got any food in there?' He pointed at the rucksack.

'Four bruised apples and four pieces of now very squashed hummingbird cake,' Jacinta replied.

'Can I have some?' Lucas whispered, while studying the ground. 'Please?'

Jacinta stared at him. 'What did you say?'

'Doesn't matter – you're not going to give it to me anyway.' He turned and began to walk away.

'Hey, come back here,' Jacinta demanded. 'If you want some cake, that is.'

Lucas stopped. He turned and saw Jacinta sit on the ground and open the backpack.

She rummaged around in the bag. 'Well, do you want some or not?'

Lucas walked back towards her and sat down.

'Here.' She handed him a piece of cake. 'I might as well have some too.' Jacinta began to unwrap a second piece. 'So, tell me what happened after you punched the bully in the nose?' she asked.

By the time Jacinta licked the last crumbs of cake from her fingers the two of them realized that they might just have quite a lot more in common than they could ever have imagined.

Chapter 23

'Oh hello, what a lovely surprise,' said Alice-Miranda as she turned around to see Lucas entering the cubby through the droopy branch door.

'What do *you* want?' Jasper rolled his eyes and backed away.

'Ugh. I'm out of here.' Lucas turned to go.

'Oh no you don't.' Jacinta put her hands on his shoulders and turned him back around. 'He's with me,' she said and gave him a little shove forward into the cubby.

Alice-Miranda raced over to hug her friend. 'I'm so glad you're better. You've been missing all the fun.' She looked at the unlikely pair. 'Is everything all right?'

'Yes, everything's fine. I told Lucas that he could come and play with us, if he wanted to,' Jacinta said firmly.

'Of course. Lucas, you're most welcome to join us – isn't he, Jasper?' Alice-Miranda said meaningfully. Jasper reluctantly nodded. 'I've been hoping to get to know you better, Lucas. It seems silly that we shouldn't be friends when we all live in the same place – don't you agree?'

Lucas managed a nod followed by a tight half smile.

'Well, this is our cubby. Isn't it amazing? We made it last year and we found all the furniture in the barn behind Rose Cottage. Mr Greening helped bring it down here in the trailer. I think it's the most gorgeous secret hideaway – just perfect for adventures. You know, I think there could even be some magic down here under this old tree,' Alice-Miranda mused.

Lucas moved away from the doorway towards the beaten accordion perched on the sideboard. 'Does that work?' he asked, pointing at the shabby relic.

'Well, it's certainly seen better days but I think it should still play a tune,' Alice-Miranda replied. 'Try it – if you want to, of course.'

Lucas picked up the accordion and gave it a squeeze. A gush of air raced out and the most awful sound followed. The children all looked at each other – and laughed.

'I think you should play us a concert,' Jacinta said, clapping her hands.

Even Jasper couldn't help but smile.

'Yes, Lucas – a concert please,' Alice-Miranda urged.

Lucas squeezed again and pressed the keys – this time the accordion sounded like a cross between a strangled cat and a windy cow. The children fell about giggling – Lucas too.

That afternoon they had the most wonderful time. Alice-Miranda had all but forgotten about the things that were troubling her. Jasper tried hard not to talk to his cousin but after a while he thawed a little. Lucas, it seemed, could be quite charming when he wasn't being horrid.

Chapter 24

Up at the Hall there was a flurry of activity. During the week the house had been cleaned from top to bottom and that afternoon there were vans and trucks delivering all manner of things from flowers and fruit to helium balloons.

'I do wish you would let me cook for the party, ma'am,' Mrs Oliver tutted as she motioned for another box of groceries to be taken to the pantry.

'Oh Dolly, nonsense, this party is for family – and

if you were cooking all day and night you wouldn't be able to enjoy it,' Cecelia reprimanded.

'But Mrs Smith is here to help me now – she arrived from the school this morning. You should have seen us there – we were a grand team. I'm sure we could have things ready in no time,' Mrs Oliver protested.

'I know you could. But really, at so many of our parties you don't have a second to join us – and it *is* Charlotte's birthday and she'd be very cross with me if you were down here slaving over hot ovens. Besides, Mummy has sent over some lovely dresses for you and Shilly and Mrs Smith to choose from – and there are matching jewels too. You know she'd be terribly offended if you were to don an apron over the top of a Valentino!'

Mrs Oliver smiled. 'Thank you, ma'am. I'm sure it will be a wonderful evening – but just don't look at me when the beef is overcooked,' she scoffed and strode to the door to take charge of yet another delivery.

Cecelia smothered a smile. 'Are the children back yet?' she asked. 'It's getting late and I don't want Jacinta catching another chill. I'm so glad she's feeling better – I was rather thinking she was about to have another awful holiday.'

Cecelia walked out onto the porch just in time to see Alice-Miranda and Jacinta striding arm in arm across the lawn. Their timing couldn't have been more perfect. A battered Land Rover lurched up the driveway and clattered to a halt outside the front steps.

'Hello darlings,' Cecelia called. 'You're just in time.'

The driver of the Land Rover got out carefully and retrieved a walking stick from the centre console. Before he reached the passenger door a very small child with red hair and glasses leaped out onto the gravel and raced towards the girls.

'Millie!' Alice-Miranda squealed and ran towards her friend. 'What are you doing here? I thought you were spending the holidays at home.' The children hugged tightly.

Millicent Jane McLoughlin-McTavish-McNoughton-McGill was Alice-Miranda's best friend and room mate at school. Although Millie was three years older than Alice-Miranda, the two girls had quickly discovered they had much in common and indeed it was hard for Millie to believe that Alice-Miranda was still only just over seven.

Cecelia walked down and greeted Millie's grandfather. 'Hello Ambrose.' She leaned forward and gave the old man a peck on both cheeks. 'Thank you so much for bringing her over. I knew Alice-Miranda and Jacinta would be thrilled. I've had to work hard not to let the cat out of the bag several times.'

'It's my pleasure, Cecelia dear. It's lovely to see you,' Ambrose McLaughlin-McTavish replied. 'She arrived yesterday and it's been such a treat to have her with me. You know, I haven't enjoyed ice-cream for breakfast in years but Millicent convinced me that it was what we both needed this morning, so we strolled down to the village and sat in the tea rooms and that's just what we ordered. I think Mrs Finch was rather disapproving but by golly it made me feel young again – and anyone who can do that for a man of my advanced years is a wonder.'

Cecelia had arranged with Millie's parents for her to stay for the rest of the holidays. As it turned out, Millie's grandfather lived only a couple of miles away and had been a friend of Cecelia's father long ago.

'Have you time for tea?' Cecelia asked.

'Is Dolly in?' Ambrose smiled.

Cecelia grinned back at him. 'She's been looking forward to seeing you all day.' Ambrose offered Cecelia his arm and together they walked inside.

'Come on girls,' she called over her shoulder. 'Why don't you take Millie up and get her settled.'

The children were laughing and chattering like monkeys.

'Mummy, this is the best surprise,' Alice-Miranda called to her mother. 'Thank you.'

And with that the girls raced through the kitchen door and flew up the back stairs. Mrs Shillingsworth was in the hallway balancing a skyscraping pile of towels.

'Girls,' she called. 'I've had to do some reshuffling with your sleeping arrangements. We have a house full of people for the weekend, so Jacinta, I'm afraid I've reclaimed your room for some of the grown-ups. But Mr Greening's been busy in your room, Alice-Miranda. I imagine you'll all approve.'

'I'm sure it will be wonderful, Shilly,' Alice-Miranda agreed. 'This is Millie,' she said, gesturing to her friend.

Mrs Shillingsworth nodded her head and said hello.

'It's a pleasure to meet you,' Millie beamed.

'Come on, everyone.' Alice-Miranda skipped down the hallway to her bedroom. She pushed open the door. 'It looks just like school,' she laughed.

The room now had three beds. Alice-Miranda's own enormous four-poster stood in the middle of the floor as always but there were now two single beds jutting out from the opposite wall under the windows.

'This is the best holiday ever!' Alice-Miranda collapsed backwards onto her bed.

Jacinta and Millie each claimed one of the single beds.

'So.' Millie rolled onto her stomach and propped herself up on her elbows. 'What have you been doing this week?'

'We've got heaps to tell you,' Jacinta began, her eyes widening.

'Yes, it's certainly been an interesting time,' Alice-Miranda agreed. 'Not quite what I had expected, but that's part of the fun, I suppose.'

Chapter 25

'So what *do* you think Mr Ridley was doing out in the garden in the middle of the night?' Millie rolled onto her back and stared at the swirling patterned plaster ceiling in Alice-Miranda's room. Jacinta had just finished telling her about the gorgeous Mr Ridley and his curious midnight meeting.

'I'm sure there's a perfectly good explanation,' Alice-Miranda replied.

'Come on, you've got to be kidding,' Jacinta rebuked. 'And what about that black car and the noises you heard when you were visiting Granny Bert and the fact that Daisy looked upset when we saw her at the start of the week. There's something strange going on around here. Even I know that and I've spent most of the week sick in bed. And then there's Lucas.'

'Well, I think he's changed a lot. He was lovely this afternoon and even Jasper seemed to be coming around to him,' Alice-Miranda replied.

'He told me some things when I fell over him in the field,' said Jacinta, who was lying flat on her bed with her legs pointed up at right angles, flexing her feet back and forth.

'What do you mean, fell over him?' Millie wrinkled her nose.

'Oh, that's not important.' Jacinta waved her hand dismissively. 'I asked him where his mother was and he said that she had gone away for work and that's why he'd been sent to boarding school. It's true what Poppy said – he was expelled but he said it was for sticking up for some poor kid who couldn't defend himself. It sounds like his mother goes away a lot. Come to think of it, I know how he feels. My mother's never around is she?' There was a sharpness in Jacinta's voice. 'When I asked about his father he got really snappy. He said he doesn't even know who he is. That's pretty sad, don't you think?'

Alice-Miranda silently admitted to herself that there were more than a few things still bothering her. But until she could talk to Mr Ridley and Lily she didn't want to let her imagination run away with itself. There had to be a perfectly sensible explanation for everything – she just couldn't work out what it was yet. And as for Granny's friend with the black car, Daisy said that everything was just fine. Granny *was* getting rather old these days, after all. She probably just mistook the plans for something else and popped them in the crisper. She'd just as likely put them away again before Alice-Miranda had returned the other day. Alice-Miranda made a mental note to check the oven the next time she was at Rose Cottage.

There was a loud knock on the door and her mother entered.

'Hello girls, I do hope your sleeping arrangements are up to scratch.' Cecelia stood in the middle of the room surveying the new layout. 'It looks rather fun to me. Do you want to come downstairs? Your grandfather is heading off soon, Millie – although I must say he and Mrs Oliver have been enjoying a lovely chat over their tea and scones.'

'Yes, Grandpa mentioned a few times as we were driving over that he hoped Mrs Oliver would be home. Apparently they were friends a long time ago, I think even before he met Granny.'

'Yes, they've been having a wonderful catch-up.' Cecelia winked at Alice-Miranda. 'I've asked if he would like to come back for dinner tomorrow night but he said something about his favourite show being on the telly.'

'Oh, that's just sad,' Millie scoffed. 'I'll have a word to him. He's become so dull since Granny passed away. He really needs to get out more. You should have seen him this morning when we went to the village and ate ice-cream for breakfast – he was making jokes and having the most wonderful time.'

'Well, come on then, girls.' Cecelia guided her charges towards the kitchen stairs. 'I'll just pop up and see how Mrs Shillingsworth is getting on, and then I'll be down in a tick.'

In the kitchen, Ambrose and Mrs Oliver were having a very jolly time when they were interrupted by the children. They were laughing so hard there were tears traversing the lines of their wizened cheeks.

'My goodness!' exclaimed Alice-Miranda. 'What's so funny?'

'Oh, oh, my dear—' Mrs Oliver disintegrated into a fit of giggles.

'Well, you see.' Ambrose almost choked on his words. 'I was reminding Dolly about a picnic rally we went on a very long time ago.' He began to chuckle.

'Yes?' Millicent walked up and put her hands on her grandfather's heaving shoulders. 'Go on, Pa,' she begged.

'Well,' Mrs Oliver snorted. 'There was a group of us heading off on a car rally, with the goal being to meet up and have a picnic lunch. I was the navigator and your grandfather here had paired me up with his best friend, Dougal. We headed off with the picnic in the back and the map in my hand. I have to say that my heart was somewhat aflutter . . .' Her chest began to heave and Dolly was again overcome with laughter.

'Did you fancy Dougal?' Millie asked.

'Rather, my dear.' Mrs Oliver composed herself.

'But that doesn't sound funny at all,' Jacinta frowned. 'What happened – why are you laughing?'

Ambrose began again. 'Well, you know that the aim of a car rally is to find a range of locations and then the final destination. Dolly wasn't very good at reading the map and after missing the first three checkpoints the rest of the party started to get a little concerned about them.'

'Where were you, Mrs Oliver?' Alice-Miranda asked.

'Oh my dear, I was trying to be very clever and decided that we should take a shortcut. There was a bit of track and we were heading to a village I knew well. So I directed Dougal down into a field. We were bumping along having the loveliest chat when out of the corner of my eye I noticed a big black bull heading towards us. It seemed that he had taken exception to our little car invading his territory. He charged right at us, snorting and pawing at the ground.'

'What happened next?' Alice-Miranda asked, wide-eyed.

'Well, we continued until the bull had his nose right up against the front of the car. He actually butted against us a few times and Dougal was rather cross about the brute damaging his paintwork. Poor Dougal put the car into reverse but only managed to bump back into a huge mud puddle. The wheels started spinning and there we were. Stuck in the mud – bogged – with this enormous beast bellowing at the top of its lungs. There was nothing we could do but sit in the field and wait to be rescued.'

'Did you find them, Pa?' Millie asked her grandfather.

'We sent a search party and in the end we were so worried they had driven off a cliff or into a river that we got the local constable involved.'

'Then what happened?' Jacinta begged.

'Well, we were there for hours! At about eight o'clock a light came into view. Sure enough there was a police car, siren blaring, heading towards us. The bull had gone to sleep in front of the car and the constable found us eating cucumber sandwiches and drinking cold sweet tea. He shooed the bull away as though it were a lamb – made Dougal and me look more than a little silly. My mother and father were quite beside themselves thinking that Dougal had made off with me. It was most improper. It was a wonder that we ever married.'

'So Dougal was your husband?' Jacinta asked.

'Yes dear, God rest his soul,' Mrs Oliver smiled.

When Millie suggested that her grandfather come back for dinner tomorrow evening, he rather surprised everyone.

'That would be delightful,' he agreed. 'Now what about that tour of your laboratory before I head off?' Ambrose guided Dolly by the arm. 'I'd love to see what you get up to down there.'

'Oh my sainted aunt!' Mrs Oliver declared. 'I've left Mrs Smith down there for hours. What a frightful friend I am!' Mrs Oliver grabbed a wooden spoon from the kitchen bench and handed it to Alice-Miranda. 'Darling girl – can you stir that pot on the stove? I'll be back as soon as I can.' And with that she raced out the door to the entrance of the cellar at the end of the veranda.

'Bye Pa,' Millie called to her grandfather as he disappeared after her.

He ducked his head back inside the door. 'Bye darling, see you tomorrow.'

Millie ran to give the old man a hug.

Chapter 26

'Well hello,' Mrs Smith greeted her red-faced friend. 'I was beginning to think you'd been kidnapped.'

'Doreen, my dear, I am terribly sorry. I've had a visitor this afternoon and we got a bit carried away with a trip down memory lane,' Mrs Oliver apologised.

Ambrose had followed her down into the cellar, albeit carefully as his legs weren't what they used to be.

'Mrs Smith, I'd like you to meet my friend, Ambrose McLoughlin-McTavish, grandfather of Alice-Miranda's little friend Millie.'

The old man extended his hand, which Mrs Smith shook gently.

'A pleasure to meet you, sir,' Mrs Smith smiled, 'I think I may have seen you up at the school.'

'And you too.' His eyes twinkled kindly. 'Yes, I like to pop over and watch Millicent play sport as often as I can manage.'

Ambrose studied the rows of stainless steel benches lined with all manner of flasks, beakers and other scientific equipment. At the other end of the cavernous room, a full commercial kitchen boasting two gigantic cookers took up a considerable amount of space. Another row of benches ran along the wall, topped by several computers.

'So what exactly do you do down here in this amazing cave, Mrs Oliver?'

'I like to invent things,' she answered.

'Oh, get off with you, woman. She's far too modest,' Mrs Smith scoffed. 'Have you heard of FDF?'

Ambrose rested his chin in his hand. 'Didn't I read something about that in the newspaper recently? FDF, now what does that stand for again?'

'Freeze-Dried Foods,' Mrs Smith replied. 'Our Dolly here is the inventor – it's all her handiwork.

But if you can think of a better name, do let us know. We're all racking our brains to come up with something more interesting, aren't we, Mrs Oliver?'

Dolly nodded.

'Goodness me, my dear. What a clever old bird you are! Who would have thought?'

Mrs Oliver blushed a deep shade of red. 'It's just something I've been playing with for a while now. The idea of having proper food, freeze-dried so that it won't perish and can be easily transported – well, after what happened to my dear Dougal, it was a challenge I couldn't resist.'

'Ah Dougal, God rest his soul.' Ambrose made a sign of the cross.

Dolly's explorer husband Dougal had met an untimely end on one of his expeditions after his food supply had run out and he was stuck in the middle of one of the worst blizzards Europe had ever seen.

'Well, you are a trick,' Ambrose said admiringly. 'And Mrs Smith, what is your role in all of this?'

'I've just come to give Dolly a helping hand for a few days while the girls are on holidays. I have no brain for inventing but I can follow instructions and am happy to assist wherever I can,' Mrs Smith replied.

'And what's that through there?' Ambrose pointed to an area at the other end of the room panelled off by thick, grey-tinted glass.

'Oh, that's where Mr Kennington-Jones keeps the most important stock – the wine, of course.' Dolly smiled and touched a fingertip to the side of her nose.

'But I thought the wine cellar was accessed from the pantry at the end of the kitchen?' Mrs Smith frowned.

'Oh no, you must be confused.' Mrs Oliver shook her head. 'Anyway, we should get back to the children. They'll be waiting for their supper.' Mrs Oliver motioned for Ambrose and Mrs Smith to go on ahead of her. She flicked the light switch and pulled the heavy metal door closed. A light on the electronic pad at the entrance flickered and she hastily punched in a series of numbers. The door shut tight and there was a sound of air rushing out.

Mrs Smith couldn't help wondering why her friend had lied about the cellar. She herself had seen it – through a passage and down some stairs in the pantry off the end of the kitchen. The glassed-off area was nothing to do with Mr Kennington-Jones's extensive wine collection at all. But then again, she didn't know what was in there either and Mrs Oliver likely had good reason to keep it a secret.

The ladies bid goodbye to Ambrose, who set off in his rattly Land Rover, vowing to return the next evening.

The children had set the table in the kitchen and were now watching television with Shilly and Cecelia in the small sitting room.

'Dolly,' Shilly called when she heard the screen door open. 'Dolly, you must come and see this. It's just ghastly.'

Mrs Oliver and Mrs Smith bustled into the room to catch the tail end of the news story.

'All those little children starving – goodness, there must be something can be done.' Shilly shook her head.

'What about FDF, Mrs Oliver?' Alice-Miranda asked. 'I thought Daddy was working on contracts with some governments.'

'Yes, darling girl – your father has been busy – but these things just take such a long time, I'm afraid,' Mrs Oliver replied.

'And then there are the people more interested in making money than anything else,' Mrs Smith added.

'Yes, like Alethea's horrid father. I read some-where that one of Addison Goldsworthy's oil mines poisoned a whole river and lots of people got very sick. If he's anything like Alethea, it probably didn't bother him one bit, as long as he got richer,' Millie added.

Alethea Goldworthy's father was one of the richest men in the world. He had made his money mining for oil and gold and just about any other precious commodity – and had quite an appalling reputation for caring little about his employees. He was even said to be on first name terms with several of the world's worst dictators.

Shilly flicked off the television.

'Well, I don't know about anyone else, but I think we need to have dinner and then I would love some help finishing off upstairs. What do you say, girls? Do you think you could give me a hand?'

'Of course . . . yes . . . what do you want us to do?' the children chorused.

'Let's talk about that in a minute, shall we? Now off you go and wash your hands.'

Chapter 27

After dinner, Alice-Miranda, Millie and Jacinta followed Cecelia to the third floor. Off the broad hallway with its pretty gold wallpaper there were eight bedrooms, including Alice-Miranda's parents' own. Cecelia explained that they were having quite a few guests for the weekend and so the group was on 'final inspection' duty for Shilly, which meant checking that there were towels in all the bathrooms, fresh flowers in the bedrooms and not a crease or wrinkle on any of the duvets. The girls were rather enjoying their jobs, eagerly ticking off the list that Shilly had sent with them. Alice-Miranda knew, however, that while this was called 'final inspection' it would be Mrs Shillingsworth who would do the final, *final* inspection after everyone was tucked up in bed.

'Mummy, why is Aunty Gee's room on this list?'

Alice-Miranda was quite used to having a house full of visitors as her parents often entertained at home, but the suite at the very end was strictly off limits to everyone except Aunty Gee – and it had been that way for as long as anyone could remember.

'Is she coming for the weekend?' Alice-Miranda asked.

Cecelia frowned. 'Well, darling, you know that we are having some people to stay. But it's a little bit more than that, actually.'

'Yes Mummy, I know. It's a surprise – for Aunt Charlotte,' Alice-Miranda smiled.

'Oh darling, however did you guess?' Cecelia pouted.

'Well, you don't usually have half the village up to help with the cleaning unless there's a special event – and there have been so many deliveries too,' Alice-Miranda noted.

Cecelia straightened a painting on the wall as she spoke. 'You don't miss much, do you?'

'I can't wait,' said Alice-Miranda and hugged her mother.

'But you mustn't say anything to Charlotte.' Cecelia looked each of the girls in the eye. 'She thinks we're just having a small get-together with Lawrence and everyone here at home.'

The party was planned for the following evening. Charlotte would be home in the morning and to keep her out of the house while the guests arrived, Lawrence had suggested when he was there earlier in the week that he would try to convince her to take a lovely long ride to a couple of the neighbouring villages.

'Now that you're all in on the plan, you can help make sure that Charlotte stays away until everything is in place,' Cecelia announced.

There was a loud creaking noise and Alice-Miranda turned to see her father arriving at the top of the stairs.

'Hello Daddy.'

Hugh Kennington-Jones did not reply. He seemed quite lost in his own thoughts.

'Helllllllooooooo Daaaadddddy,' Alice-Miranda called again in a singsong voice.

Hugh jolted as if surprised and turned towards the girls. 'Oh, hello darling.' He walked towards the group at the end of the hallway. 'Sorry, I was far, far away,' he apologised. 'Hello Millie – lovely to see you again.' He reached down and gave her a hug. Then he stepped back and looked at Jacinta. 'And how are you feeling, young lady? You're certainly looking much better.'

'I'm fine, thank you,' Jacinta replied.

'And we're all so excited about Aunt Charlotte's party,' said Alice-Miranda as she put her tiny hand into her father's and the group walked back towards the top of the stairs.

'I thought we were keeping that a surprise,' Hugh scolded Cecelia.

'Yes, well, we were, but you know this one' – she rolled her eyes affectionately and pointed at Alice-Miranda – 'has a habit of asking just the right questions.'

The grandfather clock on the landing began to chime.

'All right, girls. It's late and you'd better get off to bed. I'll come down and tuck you in soon,' Cecelia instructed as the clock struck nine.

'Goodnight Daddy,' said Alice-Miranda.

Hugh lifted her into his arms and gave her a kiss

on the cheek. She kissed him back again as she always did. It was their bedtime game.

'Love you.' She pressed her cheek against his, and then rubbed her face with her hand, objecting to his evening stubble. 'You need a shave, Daddy.'

'No, I don't think so,' he teased. 'Perhaps I'll grow a beard.'

'No, *I* don't think so.' Cecelia shook her head.

'Me either.' Alice-Miranda wrinkled her nose. 'Beards are awful.'

Hugh put Alice-Miranda down.

'Goodnight.' Millie and Jacinta waved.

'Can we show Millie the rollercoaster ride tomorrow?' Jacinta asked as the girls walked three-across down the stairs.

'You have a rollercoaster?' Millie gasped.

'Well, sort of,' Alice-Miranda smiled. 'Not quite what you think, but a lot of fun.'

'I'm up for it,' Millie enthused.

'Yes, perhaps we can have a turn tomorrow?' Jacinta ran her fingers down the highly polished balustrade and winked at Alice-Miranda.

'Maybe.' Alice-Miranda winked back.

Meanwhile, Hugh and Cecelia headed into their bedroom.

'So, how was your day?' Cecelia asked as Hugh slipped his jacket off and began to undo his tie.

'I've had better,' he sighed, walking into the spacious wardrobe.

'Why? What happened?' Cecelia called.

'It's the FDF contracts. I thought we were ready to sign the deal but apparently there's another player about to enter the market. Hector Baines called me this afternoon to say that there had been mutterings about someone else having an identical product and now the governments aren't willing to sign anything until they meet with this new supplier.' Hugh walked back into the bedroom.

Hector Baines, the CEO of Care Planet, had been negotiating contracts with several Third World governments, having seen the incredible results of the FDF trials. He was anxious to get things signed and delivered as quickly as possible.

'So who's this new supplier?' Cecelia asked.

'That's just it. Nobody's talking. I have no idea,' Hugh replied. 'As far as I'm aware, no one else has come close to Mrs Oliver's formula.'

'Well, I'm sure it will work out,' Cecelia reassured him. 'I'd better pop down and tuck the girls in. You should see Alice-Miranda's room. It looks like the school dorm.' She kissed her husband on the top of his head as he sat at the writing desk scanning the afternoon paper.

'Say goodnight from me.' Hugh didn't look up as his eyes locked onto a small article in the bottom left-hand corner of page eight. The headline read GOLDSWORTHY INDUSTRIES ENTERS FOOD RELIEF MARKET – A HELPING HAND FOR ALL . . .

'You've got to be kidding me,' Hugh muttered.

'What was that, darling?' Cecelia leaned back inside the doorway.

'Nothing, Cee. Nothing at all,' he lied.

Chapter 28

At breakfast on Friday, Alice-Miranda asked what time her aunt and Mr Ridley would be arriving. Just as her mother opened her mouth to reply there was the sound of crunching gravel on the driveway and the low rumbling of a sports car engine.

'She's here!' Alice-Miranda leaped from her chair, ran to the kitchen door and raced outside to greet her beloved aunt.

'Goodness me, now there's a welcome you don't get every day.' Charlotte lifted herself from the passenger seat and scooped Alice-Miranda into her arms. Alice-Miranda kissed Charlotte's cheeks and forehead and lastly the tip of her nose.

'How is my favourite only niece?' Charlotte manoeuvred Alice-Miranda onto her left hip. 'I think you've grown – you're getting much too heavy to be carried about.'

Alice-Miranda frowned momentarily, and then smiled.

'You *can* put me down. I've grown a centimetre since I started at my new school,' Alice-Miranda proudly told her aunt.

'A whole centimetre – is that all? I thought it must be at least five.' Charlotte knelt down to meet Alice-Miranda's big brown eyes.

People often said that Alice-Miranda was the image of her Aunt Charlotte when she was little. Both had the same cascading chocolate curls and brown eyes as big as saucers. They shared much the same attitude to life too. Charlotte headed up the public relations team for Highton's and it was often remarked that there was no one she couldn't win over – eventually.

'So what do you have planned for me this weekend?' Charlotte stood up and held Alice-Miranda's hand.

'Tons of things – but you'll have just have to wait and see.'

Lawrence was retrieving their bags from the boot of the car.

'Hello Mr Ridley,' Alice-Miranda smiled. 'It's nice to see you again.'

Lawrence pressed his right forefinger to his lips.

'Oops,' Alice-Miranda breathed as she remembered that she was not supposed to say anything about his being at the house earlier in the week.

'Again?' Charlotte interjected. 'I didn't think you'd met Lawrence before.'

'What I meant to say is, I'm very pleased to meet you.' Alice-Miranda strode forward and offered him her hand.

Lawrence shook it gently.

'And it's a pleasure to meet you too. It's Alice-Miranda, isn't it?' Lawrence winked slyly.

'I suppose it's easy to think that I know Mr Ridley because I've see him in movies and things,' said Alice-Miranda to cover her tracks.

'Yes, I suppose so,' Charlotte laughed. 'I must admit that to me he's just my lovely Lawrie.' He kissed her playfully on the cheek. 'I didn't realize you were popular with the pre-teen set.'

'Hello darling,' Cecelia called from the veranda. 'Come on in. Dolly's put the pot on and I think there could be pancakes if you hurry.'

Charlotte greeted her sister with an enthusiastic hug. 'It's so good to be here. I always feel better as soon as I see the chimneypots.'

In the kitchen, introductions were made. Alice-Miranda was relieved that Jacinta had obviously remembered that she wasn't to let on anything about meeting Mr Ridley earlier in the week. Perhaps her parents had reminded her before he came inside. Jacinta was obviously still besotted with Lawrence. Her eyes glazed over as soon as he entered the room.

Breakfast was a jolly affair. Mrs Oliver, Mrs Smith and Shilly joined the family at the kitchen table. Shilly didn't even protest that she still had a million things to do; she was afraid that if she raced off it would arouse Charlotte's suspicions.

'Charlotte, I've put you in the yellow room and Mr Ridley, you're in the blue room adjacent,' said Shilly, glancing at the happy couple. 'Your mother will be arriving later this morning and I've popped her in the rose bedroom on the top floor.'

'That's lovely, thanks Shill,' Charlotte replied.

'Well, I must get off and do some jobs,' Shilly said, rising and tucking her chair away.

'What are you getting up to for the rest of the day?' Hugh asked Lawrence and Charlotte.

'Well,' Lawrence began, 'Charlotte and I have spoken and I thought, if it was all right with you, that we might take a couple of horses and go for a long ride. I've heard there are some pretty villages close by and I'd love to have a bit of a gander.'

'It will be such fun,' Charlotte enthused. 'I haven't been riding in ages and I miss the horses so much. What about the girls – would you like to come with us?'

'Yes please!' Alice-Miranda jumped up and threw her arms around Charlotte's neck.

'Darling, I think you'd better ask Millie and Jacinta what they feel like doing,' Cecelia chided.

'Sorry Mummy, it's just that I haven't seen Aunt Charlotte in ages. Do you want to go riding?' Alice-Miranda asked her friends.

'I'd love to,' Millie replied.

'No thanks.' Jacinta wrinkled her nose. 'But I'd be quite happy to stay here and do some stretching and then perhaps a bit of tumbling on the front lawn. The flu really wrecked my training schedule and I should get back to it. I wouldn't mind going for a run either.'

'We won't go, Jacinta. It's not fair for you to be by yourself all day.' Alice-Miranda sat back down on her chair.

'Don't stay for me,' Jacinta replied. 'I'll be fine and if I get lonely I can always go and find Jasper and Poppy.'

'Mummy, what do you think?' Alice-Miranda turned to face her mother.

'Well, Jacinta if that's really OK with you, then I think it would be lovely for Alice-Miranda and Millie to join Lawrie and Cha. It's such a beautiful day. Daddy and I have some work to do so why don't you all head off and get ready,' Cecelia instructed. 'But you need to be back by 5 p.m.. Dinner is set for 6 p.m. and I hope you don't mind, Charlotte, but I've asked the Greenings, Daisy and Granny and the Bauers to join us. And I think Max and Cyril might pop in too.'

'Sounds lovely,' Charlotte replied.

'I'll phone down to the stables and see if Max can get started saddling up. You take Shergar, Lawrence, and Charlotte, you can take Boo,' Hugh offered. 'And what about little Phinnie for you, Millie?'

'Sounds great,' Millie replied.

'Boo!' Charlotte exclaimed. 'Dear old Boo – I haven't ridden him for ever. Golly, if only I had enough room in town for darling old Boo to come and stay.'

'I can't imagine your neighbours would be very pleased if you turned up with an old racehorse in the back garden,' Cecelia smiled.

'A painting or a picture – that's the only way I'm going to have Boo at home in town,' Charlotte pouted.

Alice-Miranda grinned.

'What are you up to, young lady?'

'It's a secret,' Alice-Miranda beamed.

The group began to move off to prepare for the events of the day.

'I'll pack some treats,' Dolly called after them. 'But you can take care of your own lunch. I hear the Rose and Donkey have some tasty pork pies.'

'Thanks Dolly,' Charlotte called. 'See you in a tick.'

Chapter 29

With everyone out of the house, Cecelia and the staff flew into overdrive. Both the dining room and ballroom were transformed with fairy lights and massed bouquets of shiny silver and pearl helium balloons. While formal celebrations usually followed a more traditional decor, the theme for Charlotte's surprise was unmistakably a nod to the sprites and pixies she so loved as a child. At 2 p.m. the rooms were declared a triumph and the doors firmly locked. Mr Greening had been busy in the garden, too, setting up the fireworks that would later bedazzle the night sky.

Jacinta spent half an hour upstairs stretching and doing some of her breathing exercises. After a light morning tea, she set off to take a run around the estate. Mrs Oliver insisted she take a small rucksack and spare phone, just in case she tired and needed someone to pick her up. She planned to cover a large circuit – the reverse direction of the route she and Alice-Miranda had taken on their first day.

Outside, the topaz sky shimmered and the crisp autumn air stirred the emerald fields. Jacinta's jog took her down the long driveway towards the gatehouse.

As she passed through the gates, a ruby-coloured Bentley entered the driveway. She noticed that it didn't have any registration plates – which was a bit strange. The Bentley was followed closely by two Jaguars and an Aston Martin.

Jacinta ran down the laneway towards Rose Cottage. She was looking out for the mysterious black car but it wasn't parked where Alice-Miranda had described seeing it. As she rounded the bend near the cottage, Jacinta thought she heard raised voices coming from the garden. She slowed down to a walk, wondering if Lucas was having another spat with Jasper. But she soon realized that the voices did not belong to children.

'I'm begging you,' a young woman's voice pleaded.

'There's no point. I can't stop things now,' a man's voice replied.

'But what will happen?' the woman asked.

'That's out of my hands,' he hissed.

Jacinta knew she shouldn't have been listening but she couldn't resist a mystery. After seeing Mr Ridley running about in the middle of the night earlier in the week, she couldn't help wondering if he was tied up with whatever *this* was too.

Jacinta peered through the bushes but couldn't see the owners of the voices.

'Who are you spying on?' a voice hissed behind her and she almost leaped over the hedge.

'Lucas!' Jacinta's heart thumped in her chest. 'Nobody.'

'That's a lie if ever I heard one,' he smirked. 'Where's your little friend?' He looked around.

'Alice-Miranda and another one of our friends, Millie, have gone out riding,' Jacinta replied. 'I was just going for a run and then I thought I heard an argument, that's all,' she replied. 'But it was nothing. What are *you* doing?' She turned and looked at him. She noticed he was holding an envelope.

'Nothing.'

'What's that?' Jacinta pointed at the letter.

'It's from my mother,' he said.

'Is everything all right?'

'Yeah, why wouldn't it be?' he snapped.

'I was just asking.' Jacinta rolled her eyes. An uncomfortable silence divided them.

Lucas was taller than Jacinta and had a shock of dark hair. He had piercing, almost-black eyes, and for a moment, just the way he was standing, he rather reminded her of someone. She couldn't think who it was, but it struck her that he was actually very good-looking.

'Why are you staring at me like that?' Lucas demanded.

'Like what?' Jacinta pretended that she wasn't looking at him at all.

'Like I've got two heads or something,' he began.

'No I wasn't. I promise,' Jacinta protested. 'It's just that you remind me of someone but I can't work out who it is.' She changed the subject. 'Are you coming tonight?'

'Lily said something about some stupid party up at *the Hall*.' He pulled a face. 'But I'm not going. I haven't got anything to say to those people and I'm sure they haven't got anything to say to me.'

'Well, I think you should come.' Jacinta stretched her right leg out onto the low stone wall, reached forward and pulled her toes back. 'I'll talk to you, and so will Alice-Miranda and Millie.'

'Why would I want to talk to you?' Lucas kicked at a loose stone.

'You're impossible, you know,' Jacinta snapped. 'Yesterday I mistook you for a human being, but I guess I was wrong.'

'Yeah, whatever,' Lucas said. But he looked wounded.

Jacinta felt a knot tighten in her stomach. Lucas was even more complicated than she was. He could be so rude and horrible, but she didn't believe that was really who he was.

She stretched her other leg. 'Do you want to come with me now?' she asked quietly.

'Why would I want to go with you?' Lucas sneered.

'Well, I just thought it would be nice to have some company. Anyway, I'm going down to the cubby and then back around to the Hall if you change your mind.'

Jacinta began to run towards the machinery shed.

'Have you got any food?' Lucas shouted.

'What?' Jacinta turned around. 'Yes, but you're not getting any unless you can beat me,' she challenged.

'Beat *you* – are you kidding me?' Lucas took off after her. 'I was cross-country champion at my school three years in a row.' He passed her and grabbed at the backpack.

'Oh really?' Jacinta overtook him again. 'So was I. See you at the cubby!'

Chapter 30

Out on their ride, Alice-Miranda was leading Millie, Charlotte and Lawrence on a merry tour. They had taken a leisurely walk and trot to the local village of Highton Mill and then proceeded to race through Lord Tavistock's property and on to Penberthy Floss, a quaint hamlet with a general store and pub. It was here that they stopped for lunch at the Rose and Donkey, and it was here that Alice-Miranda finally had her moment alone with Mr Ridley.

'I need to go to the loo,' said Aunt Charlotte. She leaped from Boo and handed the reins to Alice-Miranda. 'All that thundering about after two cups of tea, I don't think it's good for me,' she grimaced.

'I'm coming too.' Millie handed Phinnie's reins to Mr Ridley.

'Looks like it's just you and me to get our transportation sorted,' Lawrence said with a wink. He followed Alice-Miranda with Shergar and Phinnie as she led Boo and Bony around to the back of the pub.

'We can tie them up here,' she said. 'Daddy and I often come over together. It's a lovely spot.'

Alice-Miranda loosened Bonaparte's girth strap, at which point he promptly thrust towards the water trough and took a long, slurpy drink. As he raised his head, he whinnied and managed to spit half a mouthful of slimy water all over his tiny owner.

'You brute,' she laughed. 'Just what I wanted – horse spit all over me before lunch.'

Lawrence laughed too.

'Mr Ridley,' Alice-Miranda began. 'May I ask you something?'

'Yes, of course,' he said, and continued fiddling with Shergar's saddle.

'You know when you came last weekend with Daddy – it wasn't an accident that you ran into him, was it?' she asked.

'I don't know what you mean,' said Lawrence a little uneasily.

'Well, I don't usually spy on people nor mind their business, but I know you met someone in the garden that night.' Alice-Miranda spoke gently. 'Jacinta saw you leaving the house and so she came and woke me up and then we followed you.'

'You did what?' Lawrence snapped.

'I am sorry. Jacinta wanted to tell Mummy and Daddy because she's convinced that you are up to no good but I told her that there had to be a perfectly reasonable explanation for why you were romping around in the garden after midnight. So we haven't said anything to anyone – well, except Millie, but she's very good at keeping secrets too,' Alice-Miranda prattled. 'I came to see you the next morning but you'd already gone out. The window was open and there were papers all over the floor. I promise I didn't read them . . . but I couldn't help seeing that you had a letter from someone named Kitty.'

Lawrence looked defeated. 'Yes, you're right, Alice-Miranda. It wasn't a coincidence that I ran into your father at the club, nor that I ended up at your house that night. But I promise you, there *is* a very good explanation for my behaviour.' His dark eyes met Alice-Miranda's. There was something about her, something wise and warm, which for some strange reason he suddenly wanted to tell her everything. 'If I tell you, you mustn't say a word,' Lawrence begged. It's all rather complicated and I suspect I might be about to make it even more so.'

'Of course.' Alice-Miranda listened as he shared his secrets.

A few minutes later, her round eyes were wider than ever. 'Oh,' she breathed. 'Now it all makes sense.'

Millie and Charlotte appeared at the rear door of the pub. 'Are you two ever coming inside?' Charlotte asked.

'I'm starving,' Millie called.

'We're coming,' Alice-Miranda replied, as she gave Bonaparte a rub behind his ears.

Lawrence knelt down on one knee to face Alice-Miranda. 'So, we're good?'

'Of course, Mr Ridley. Your secrets are safe with me,' she smiled.

Chapter 31

By the time the riding party arrived back at Highton Hall, everything and everyone was in place. The guests were under strict instructions to remain out of sight until 6.30 p.m. when they were to gather in the formal dining room. Their cars had been hidden behind the stables, in sheds and garages. Hugh was to bring Charlotte to the drawing room for drinks at exactly 6 p.m., via the back stairs, where just the family and staff would be waiting.

Alice-Miranda and Millie found Jacinta in

Alice-Miranda's bedroom. She was looking at the dresses Cecelia had had sent up for her and Millie to choose from.

'Hello, how was your ride?' Jacinta asked as she heard the girls come through the door.

'It was great fun,' Millie replied. 'We had a race and I won – but only by a nose – and that's only because Phinnie has the longest nose I've ever seen on a pony. I don't think she'd be in the running for any beauty contests, that's for sure,' Millie laughed.

'Poor Phinnie. I think she's beautiful anyway – and she's certainly a lot better behaved than Bonaparte,' Alice-Miranda added. 'Did you go for your run?'

'Yes. And I heard some people arguing in the garden at Rose Cottage – but it was very strange. I couldn't work out what it was about. But I think it might have something to do with Mr Ridley,' she began.

'I don't think so,' Alice-Miranda replied.

'Why? Did you ask him what he was doing out in the garden at midnight?' Jacinta sat down on the edge of her bed.

'We had a talk and I can assure you he's done nothing wrong. He asked me not to say anything and I promised.'

'Come on,' Jacinta begged. 'That's not fair. I told you about the argument at the cottage.'

'No, Jacinta, I made a promise.'

'Leave it, Jacinta,' Millie interrupted. 'We're going to a party and I for one plan to have a wonderful evening.'

'He's probably lying – just so you won't suspect anything,' Jacinta huffed and rolled her eyes. 'He's far too good-looking to be trusted, you know.'

Alice-Miranda smothered a smile and tried to distract her friend. 'Have you chosen a dress?'

'Yes – what do you think of this one?' Jacinta held up a beautiful mauve silk with a pretty round neckline and layered short sleeves that looked like petals.

'It's lovely.' Alice-Miranda walked to her wardrobe and began to look through her own clothes.

'What do you think of this one for me?' Millie picked up an emerald-coloured dress with a fitted bodice and organza skirt. There were delicate ribbon bows appliquéd around the hemline. She held it against her.

'That colour looks amazing with your hair,' Alice-Miranda enthused. 'You should definitely wear that – it's splendid.' She turned back to the wardrobe, and pulled out a pink dress with a wide white sash around the middle. It had a long layered skirt.

'And you should definitely wear that one.' Jacinta nodded at Alice-Miranda.

The girls took turns having showers and helped each other get dressed. Cecelia appeared in the most gorgeous floor-length pink gown – empire line with a black bow sitting just under the bust and the most amazing ruffled sleeves. The girls all commented that she looked like a supermodel. Hair was then dried and styled and the girls were ready to head downstairs.

Hugh Kennington-Jones met the girls in the hallway. 'Look at you lot! Turn.' His finger pirouetted, motioning for the girls to do the same. 'Lovely, lovely, lovely. You too, darling.' He took Cecelia's hand and kissed it gently. 'Beautiful.'

Hugh looked rather dashing himself. He was a striking man, with olive skin and thick salt-and-pepper hair. Dressed in a stylish dinner jacket he looked every inch the lord of the manor.

It was quarter to six. In the drawing room spirits were high as Mr and Mrs Greening, Mrs Oliver and Millie's grandfather, Mrs Smith and Mrs Shillingsworth allowed themselves to be waited on by the staff that had been hired especially for the evening. Lily and Heinrich were there too and Daisy and Granny Bert. Poppy and Jasper were wandering around the room admiring the myriad bits and pieces that had been collected over hundreds of years. Alice-Miranda's grandmother had yet to join the party but it was her trademark to be late.

Mrs Oliver turned and saw the girls and Hugh and Cecelia at the door. 'Don't you all look lovely!'

'Such pretty dresses,' Mrs Greening added.

'Is that really my granddaughter over there?' Ambrose squinted.

Millie playfully poked out her tongue, then ran to give the old man a hug. 'It's not my usual style, I know,' Millie said and curtsied. 'But it is fun to dress up once in a while.'

Alice-Miranda walked over to Jasper but was immediately pounced upon by Poppy.

'Where's Lucas?' Jacinta asked as she joined them.

'He didn't come,' Jasper replied. 'Said something about it not being his thing.'

'That's a pity,' Jacinta said and frowned. 'I thought I might have talked him into it this afternoon.'

At that moment Charlotte and Lawrence appeared in the doorway. Charlotte was beautiful in a blue Grecian-style gown and Lawrence looked every inch the movie star in his dinner jacket.

'Well, here comes the birthday girl,' Granny Bert bleated.

'It's not until tomorrow, Granny,' Charlotte said. 'But I'm so glad everyone could be here tonight to celebrate. This is wonderful.'

She moved around and said hello to everyone, introducing Lawrence too. Jacinta noticed Daisy standing on the other side of the room. Her lips were pursed and she kept looking around, as if expecting to see someone. Jacinta wondered if it might have been Daisy she had overheard in the garden.

'Hello Granny Bert, this is my friend Millie,' said Alice-Miranda.

'A pleasure to meet you, Sophie,' Granny replied. 'Perhaps you'd like to come and visit me. Alice-Miranda says that she will but she doesn't. Would you be a dear and ask that waitress over there to bring me another glass of lime and soda – I'm rather parched,' Granny complained. 'Oh and bring me my handbag, Alice-Miranda – I've left half my lipstick on the side of that glass. It's meant to stay on all day. Those cosmetic companies tell such lies.'

'I see Granny is her usual happy, mixed-up self,' Jacinta commented to Alice-Miranda.

'Wait until the dancing starts – then she'll really get going,' Alice-Miranda giggled, then headed off to find the waitress.

When Granny Highton-Smith finally arrived, Hugh walked to the centre of the room. He tapped the side of his glass and the crowd fell silent.

'Ladies and gentlemen, thank you for sharing this auspicious occasion, that being the eve of my beautiful sister-in-law's birthday. I won't tell you which one because a lady never tells her age and if her brother-in-law reveals it, he will be in serious trouble with all female members of the family – and if you haven't noticed, I am a little outnumbered.'

There was a titter of laughter around the room.

'And so, let's raise a toast to our darling Charlotte.'

'Darling Charlotte,' the room echoed.

'And now, might I suggest we head to the dining room. I don't know about you lot but I could eat a horse,' Hugh laughed.

'That's probably what you'll get,' Mrs Oliver tutted, still not quite over the fact that she hadn't been allowed to cook for the occasion.

The group moved through to the main foyer and the dining room – where the doors were still closed.

'Goodness me, Shilly,' Hugh called. 'I know you're always worried when we have new staff in but did you really need to lock the place up?' He threw her a dramatic curious glance. Charlotte was standing beside Hugh and Lawrence as he pushed open the giant cedar doors.

'SURPRISE!' the room erupted.

Charlotte was speechless. 'Oh my goodness!' She turned to her sister. 'However did you arrange all this?' She hugged Cecelia.

'Well, we thought you wouldn't mind,' Cee whispered.

'Mind? This is amazing.' Charlotte took a step forward. 'Hello everyone – hello.'

The room grew noisy as the guests talked among themselves. Charlotte moved around to greet everyone. 'Wow – I can't believe you're here . . . I thought you were still overseas . . . and you knew about this for how long?'

Alice-Miranda and the girls had been charged with the job of making everyone feel at home. Millie headed straight for a lady wearing a black gown and a ruby and diamond tiara.

'Hello, I'm Millie.' She curtsied. 'What a lovely tiara.'

'Aren't you a darling?' the woman replied. 'Please call me Aunty Gee. It's very nice to meet you, Millie.'

Millicent studied the woman's face carefully and decided that she must be Mrs Oliver's sister – they could have been twins.

The room buzzed. For the moment nobody noticed the handsome stranger talking with Daisy in the corner. Only Granny Bert recognized Mr Blunt, the man who had been writing the book about the Hall. She thought it was lovely that the Highton-Smith-Kennington-Joneses had invited him. They must have approved of his work.

Chapter 32

The room was bustling with over one hundred guests. Old family friends mingled with Charlotte's school pals and the rest of the household. Young Max looked dashing in his borrowed dinner jacket, even though he kept tugging at the bow tie and complaining to Cyril that it felt like a straitjacket. Shilly looked stunning in a navy blue gown, which was complemented by a Cartier diamond necklace borrowed from Granny Highton-Smith. Mrs Oliver wore a striking black Valentino dress with a long strand of South Sea pearls. Mrs Smith had selected a fire engine red Chanel frock, which Granny had worn once before to the opera. The entire staff looked magnificent.

Mrs Oliver could not remember ever laughing so much, as Ambrose McLaughlin-McTavish kept her well and truly amused. Mrs Smith seemed to have her hands full too as she received more than her fair share of attention from crusty old Lord Gisborne.

'So tell me,' Lord Gisborne asked. 'I hear that Mrs Oliver's been busy in the cellars lately.'

'Oh yes, she's a trick.' Mrs Smith fiddled with the stem of her champagne flute. 'I've never known such a talent – well, except perhaps Alice-Miranda. Did you know that Mrs Oliver has perfected the Freeze-Dried Foods formula? I think Mr Kennington-Jones is just about to sign contracts to have it shipped all over the world. My goodness, the woman could almost single-handedly bring an end to malnutrition and starvation. She's a genius,' Mrs Smith went on. She was far more talkative than usual.

'Fascinating,' Lord Gisborne went on. 'And I hear she does all this work in the cellars, right here under the Hall?'

'Oh yes – she has an amazing set-up. There's a

laboratory and a kitchen and computers – you name it, it's all down there.'

'I'd love to see it sometime. I hope she has those formulas locked away safely.' He grinned like a shark in a school of sardines. 'I can't imagine how valuable they must be.'

'Oh yes,' Mrs Smith began. 'She stores them all up here.' She tapped her finger to the side of her head.

'What?' Lord Gisborne's charm had left the building. 'She doesn't save them anywhere? What sort of an idiot is the woman?'

Mrs Smith was taken aback.

'Dolly Oliver is just about the smartest person I know,' Mrs Smith protested indignantly. 'And you, sir, are just plain rude.' She turned on her heel and harrumphed as she strode away.

Lord Gisborne reached into his pocket and fiddled nervously with his phone.

'Oh, for heaven's sake, Percy, put that awful thing away,' Aunty Gee chided. 'It's Charlotte's birthday party.'

Lord Gisborne did as he was told, then skulked off to another corner of the room where he hid behind a potted palm.

In the opposite corner, Rupert Blunt reached into the top pocket of his coat and retrieved his mobile phone.

'Change of plans, Daisy,' he whispered. 'Come with me.' He grabbed her hand and led her through the crowded room.

Granny Bert spied them together. 'Oh, I just *knew* he was perfect for her,' she remarked to Cecelia.

'Who are you talking about, Granny?' she asked.

'You know him, dear. The lovely man who's writing the history of the Hall, Mr Blunt.'

Cecelia shook her head, wondering what on earth she had missed.

Chapter 33

Rupert Blunt did not let go of Daisy's hand until they were out the front door and safely hidden on the western veranda.

'Curses, curses, curses!' he sat down on a bench seat, clutching his head in his hands.

'What's the matter now?' Daisy whispered. Her eyes filled with tears that threatened to spill onto her perfectly made-up face.

Blunt looked up. 'Well apparently the silly old goat doesn't have the formulas written down anywhere, does she? She keeps them all in her head, can you believe it?' He stood up and began to pace. 'This changes everything.'

Daisy stared out into the moonlit garden, her hands clenched together. 'Maybe you should just stop it now. I promise I won't tell anyone.'

'Shut up, woman. I need to think,' he snapped. 'It was meant to be simple – in and out – no complications.' His eyes narrowed. 'Now it looks like we'll need back-up. It's just as well I have you . . . for insurance.' Blunt's handsome face had taken on the appearance of a viper set for the kill.

Around the same time, Alice-Miranda, Millie and Jacinta had headed outside too. Alice-Miranda wanted to see if Lucas had changed his mind about coming over – it would be just like him to be lurking about in the garden somewhere. She led the girls around the corner of the veranda, where they spotted Daisy gazing out into the darkness. Then they caught sight of the tall man striding up and down – a look of thunder on his face.

The three girls stopped in their tracks. 'Who's that with Daisy?' Jacinta whispered.

'I don't know. But he doesn't look very happy,' Alice-Miranda replied. 'Let's go and say hello – I can't imagine why anyone would be upset at a party – especially one as lovely as this.' She skipped towards them. 'Hello Daisy. And hello – my name is Alice-Miranda Highton-Smith-Kennington-Jones and I'm very pleased to meet you, Mr . . .' She offered her tiny hand.

'Hmph?' he grunted. 'Hadn't you girls best go inside? It's getting late and you never know what might be out here.'

'Well, that's silly,' Alice-Miranda laughed. 'There is nothing out here to hurt us. I'm sorry, sir,' Alice-Miranda tried again, 'I don't think we've met before. My name is Alice-Miranda Highton-Smith-Kennington-Jones.'

'I'm not deaf,' Blunt snapped. 'I heard you perfectly well the first time.'

Millie wrinkled her nose. 'I don't know who invited you to this party but I'm sure that Alice-Miranda's parents are not friends with anyone as rude as you,' she blurted.

'Millie!' Alice-Miranda rebuked. 'I'm very sorry, sir; my friend didn't mean to upset you.' She decided to change tack. 'I love your dress, Daisy. That dandelion colour looks so beautiful with your eyes.'

Daisy managed a nervous half smile in reply. 'Thank you, sweet girl,' she whispered.

The man began to tap his foot on the flagstones. 'That's enough chitchat. Now run along. I'm sure your parents must be missing you.'

'Oh no, not at all. They're having a lovely time inside with all our friends,' Alice-Miranda cooed. 'It's such a wonderful party, isn't it? I've never seen so many beautiful dresses in the one place – well except for when Mummy took me to Paris for the fashion shows last year and Mr Valentino gave us a lovely tour of his salon.'

'Oh, for goodness sake,' Blunt interrupted. 'You girls need to go. *Now*.' His steely voice sliced the air.

Alice-Miranda's strange feeling had well and truly returned.

'Girls, please go inside,' Daisy gulped.

The man grabbed Daisy by the hand and, with cyclonic speed, he wrenched her around the corner and they were gone. By the time the girls ran to see, they had both well and truly disappeared.

'He's foul,' Jacinta said.

'I agree.' Millie nodded her head. 'Do you think he could have been one of the people you heard having the argument in the garden at Rose Cottage this afternoon? I think Daisy looked scared of him,' she added.

'He does seem a little bit upset,' Alice-Miranda said. 'Gosh grown-ups can be complicated at times.'

Alice-Miranda was now quite sure that Daisy was hiding something. She just needed to work out what it was.

Chapter 34

'Mrs Oliver,' Aunty Gee interrupted, 'may I steal you away dear?'

'Of course, ma'am.' Mrs Oliver excused herself and left Ambrose talking with Mrs Smith.

'I've heard about your remarkable work. FDF is sheer brilliance. I was rather hoping to get a tour of your laboratory – if you don't mind?'

'It would be my pleasure. What about tomorrow morning?' Mrs Oliver asked.

'Well, I'm afraid I have to be getting back to town

rather early. Frederick is throwing some dreadful garden party. I'm sure that he'll regale us with his latest theory on organic gardening . . . terribly dull, dear, but I can't bunk out of it at this late stage,' she said, rolling her eyes.

Mrs Oliver checked her watch. 'Would you like to have a look now? We could duck off for a few minutes.'

'That would be lovely,' Aunty Gee agreed. She turned to the tall, bulky man standing beside her. 'Dalton, why don't you go and keep Mr McLoughlin-McTavish entertained while I steal Dolly?'

The man gave a hint of a bow and turned back to find his charge.

Behind the potted palm, Lord Gisborne had been listening to the ladies and their chatter. He retrieved the phone from his top pocket and began tapping in a message.

The two ladies set off for the cellar, out the kitchen door and along the veranda. They teetered on their high heels down the narrow stairwell to the bottom, where Dolly punched in the alarm code. There was a whoosh of air and a loud clunk as several bolts released.

'Good to see you have security, my dear. I imagine quite a few rogues would like to get their hands on your invention,' Aunty Gee commented as she walked into the cavernous room.

Mrs Oliver flicked the light switch and the place glowed.

'What a marvellous set-up.' Aunty Gee walked around studying the beakers and flasks.

The two ladies chatted about the process Mrs Oliver used and how many failed attempts she had made before things came right.

'I imagine there's a secret ingredient or two,' Aunty Gee smiled.

'Yes, ma'am.'

'And are you working on anything new?'

'Well actually, I am – but I haven't shown anyone yet, not even Mr Kennington-Jones. Would you like to be the first to see it?' Mrs Oliver was as eager as a child in a lolly shop.

'I'd be honoured,' Aunty Gee replied.

'Oh dear, I've left the key to the vault upstairs. Do you mind if I pop up and get it?'

'Of course, dear,' Aunty Gee agreed. 'I'll just have a wander and I promise not to touch anything.'

Mrs Oliver scurried as fast as she could manage

up the stairs and into the side sitting room, where she had a secret box containing a number of keys.

In the cellar, Aunty Gee waited patiently for her to return. She observed the complex chemistry equipment and wandered around the vast kitchen with its numerous appliances. She heard footsteps on the stairs and then the lights went out.

'Are you there, dear?' Aunty Gee called.

There was a shuffling sound, followed by 'Gotcha!' Two torches clicked on and two men dressed in black stood over Aunty Gee's limp body.

'Gawd, the tiara's a bit over the top for the hired help,' the taller man scoffed. 'Who's she think she is – the Queen?'

'Let's get her out of here. Where's that passage-way?' the shorter man asked as he studied a yellowed map.

'Did you lock the door?'

'Yeah and I scrambled the pad. It'll take ages to get back into this place – and by that time we'll 'ave everything we need.'

'And this one' – he grinned a toothless smile at Aunty Gee – 'will be long gone.'

Dolly descended the stairs to the cellar. She was surprised to find the door shut. A sick feeling engulfed her when she punched in the alarm sequence and nothing happened. 'Ma'am?' she called. But there was no answer. 'Ma'am, are you in there?'

The door must be stuck, she thought. This was no time to panic – although this had never happened before. She would go and find Mr Kennington-Jones. He would know exactly what to do.

Chapter 35

Alice-Miranda, Jacinta and Millie headed back to the dining room via the kitchen, where a tray of chocolate mousses diverted their attention. Alice-Miranda had just finished placing three of the delicious desserts on the kitchen table when the outside door flew open and Mrs Oliver barrelled inside, knocking a young waiter carrying a tray of drinks sideways. Several flutes and goblets teetered then crashed one after the other onto the flagstone floor.

'Goodness. Are you all right, Mrs Oliver?'

Alice-Miranda leaped forward and offered the woman her arm. 'Come and sit down.'

'Oh, look what I've done. I'm terribly sorry,' she apologised to the wine-splattered lad whose white shirt now looked like evidence that he'd been attacked by a savage beast. 'You'll find yourself another shirt in the pantry, dear boy. I am sorry.'

Another young girl from the catering team began to help him clear up the mess on the floor.

Mrs Oliver caught her breath. 'I'm fine. I just need to find your father.'

'Well, you don't look fine,' Millie replied.

'You look like you've seen a ghost,' Jacinta added. 'Have you?' Her eyes widened.

'No, no, my dear, I have not seen a ghost. It's just the door to the laboratory. I need to get your father, Alice-Miranda,' Mrs Oliver insisted.

'What about the door?' Alice-Miranda asked. 'I'm sure we could help you with whatever it is that's the matter.'

'I'll get you a drink of water,' Jacinta offered.

She picked up a bottle of clear liquid from the sideboard, quickly poured a large tumbler full and offered it to Mrs Oliver, who gulped it down without taking a breath. Then, like jelly on a plate, she shuddered from the tips of her toes to the top of her head.

'Where did that come from?' Mrs Oliver motioned at the empty glass. 'Because I can tell you now that was not water, my dear.'

'Over there.' Jacinta pointed towards the sink where she had left the empty bottle.

'Ughhhh!' Mrs Oliver's tongue flicked in and out like a snake's. 'That, my dear, was a rather ghastly mixture of shark liver oil, boiled essences of lavender and chamomile and a range of secret ingredients I've been developing as a relaxant. I wonder how it found its way out of the pantry.'

'Oops, sorry,' Jacinta apologised, before she walked over to the sink, where this time she poured a glass of water straight from the tap.

Alice-Miranda pulled a chair around to sit beside Mrs Oliver, who was looking remarkably more relaxed already. A hint of colour had returned to her cheeks and the wrinkles on her brow were beginning to flatten out.

'So, what's the problem?' Alice-Miranda asked again.

'Well, it's the door. It's stuck. I was showing Aunty Gee about and now she doesn't seem to be able to hear me to release the emergency lock,' Mrs Oliver babbled.

'So, the door's stuck and Aunty Gee's in the cellar,' Alice-Miranda repeated. 'Well, I'm sure that she'll find her way out. She's very smart, you know. She always beats me at draughts,' Alice-Miranda smiled and put her arm around Mrs Oliver's shoulders.

The woman nodded. 'Is your father in the dining room?'

'I think so. Millie, can you and Jacinta run and find Daddy and we'll go back downstairs and work on the door?' Alice-Miranda directed.

'Of course.' Millie licked a sliver of chocolate from her lips. 'Come on Jacinta.' She grabbed the other girl, then turned and pointed at the remnants of her chocolate mousse. 'And I'll be back for you later.'

'Come on.' Alice-Miranda took Mrs Oliver's hand in hers. 'Let's go and open that silly old door.'

At the bottom of the stairs, the keypad blinked at them, its red eye pulsing in time with Mrs Oliver's pounding heart.

'Can you remember the combination?' Alice-Miranda asked.

'Yes, yes, but I've tried that already and it doesn't appear to be working,' Mrs Oliver replied. Her face was the colour of cold custard.

There was a clattering on the stairs and Jacinta and Millie appeared with Alice-Miranda's father in tow.

'Oh Dolly, whatever are you doing? You really shouldn't be working tonight. I'm sure Ambrose is missing you upstairs,' Hugh tutted.

Mrs Oliver began to explain that she wasn't working at all. She had taken Aunty Gee for a tour of the laboratory but popped back upstairs to get the key to the vault as she was going to give her a preview of her new project.

'What is it?' Hugh asked.

'What's what, sir?' Dolly quizzed.

'The new project, of course.'

'It's a super preservation gene in organic vegetables.'

'Golly, that sounds beaut – when will it be ready?' Hugh asked, clearly impressed.

'Well, not for a while yet, sir, but that's quite beside the point,' Mrs Oliver said anxiously.

She explained that when she returned to the cellar the door was firmly locked and she wasn't able to raise Aunty Gee at all.

'So Aunty Gee is in the cellar?' Hugh repeated. 'And was Dalton with you?'

'No, sir, Aunty Gee told him to stay behind with Ambrose. She said he never gets to enjoy these things,' Mrs Oliver grimaced. 'I'm worried, sir. I think we're down to the last chance before the door shuts down completely for 24 hours.' Miniature pearls of perspiration had formed along the lines on Mrs Oliver's forehead.

'Let's think carefully about this.' Hugh stared at the keypad, drumming his fingers on the wall beside it.

'Daddy – isn't there an override combination? It has something to do with our birthdays, doesn't it?' Alice-Miranda offered.

'Yes, of course. That's it!' Mrs Oliver reached forward and punched in the eight digit number. There was a whoosh of air and a loud clunk as the bolts released. The room was in darkness.

'Well done, my clever little one.' Hugh grinned at his daughter and switched on the lights, which flickered before bursting into life.

'Oh, thank heavens.' Dolly bustled into the room with Hugh behind her.

'Aunty Gee,' Hugh called. 'Aunty Gee – are you here?'

There was no reply. The group scoured the room but there was no sign of her. Something glinted on the floor, catching Hugh's attention. He reached down to pick it up. It was a ruby – a perfect princess cut ruby. Hugh held the gem aloft.

'Wasn't Aunty Gee wearing a ruby tiara?' Alice-Miranda asked.

'Yes, she was.' Millie raced over to have a look. 'I told her it was lovely.'

Mrs Oliver spied something under the bench. It was a white cloth – and not one she recognized. Her laboratory was always in meticulous order and she never left anything lying about on the floor. As she picked it up her head began to spin and she was almost immediately overcome.

'Oh no!' Mrs Oliver dropped the cloth and exhaled. 'I hope this isn't what I think it is.'

Hugh walked over to inspect her find. 'What do you think is it?

'Chloroform,' Mrs Oliver replied.

'Chloroform!' Alice-Miranda exclaimed. 'Isn't that what they use to knock people out?'

'Well, yes, but darling, I'm sure there's a perfectly rational explanation for everything,' her father began.

'I'm not so sure.' Millie held up a piece of paper she had just found on the bench.

'Let me see that.' Jacinta snatched the paper from Millie's hand and read the words aloud. '"Once we have the formula, we might think about sending her back, but then again we might just kill her instead."'

Dolly clasped her hands to her mouth. 'Oh good heavens! They meant to take me. They want the formula.'

Hugh bit his lip. 'Yes, a bit of a problem that. I doubt there's much Aunty Gee will be able to tell them. I don't imagine she knows much about scientific formulas really. Being the Queen and all.'

'The Queen!' Millie gasped.

'So *that's* why nobody else is allowed to use her suite,' Jacinta added.

'You never told me you were friends with the Queen!' Millie stood with her mouth gaping. 'I thought she was your sister, Mrs Oliver – you look like twins. It never occurred to me that the reason she looked so familiar is that she's the Queen. But her name's Aunty Gee . . . Ohhhh,' Millie gasped, as it all became clear. 'Aunty Gee is Queen Georgiana! What's Queen Georgiana doing at Aunt Charlotte's birthday party anyway?'

'Aunty Gee is Granny Highton-Smith's best friend,' Alice-Miranda explained. 'They went to school together all the way from nursery. She's Mummy's godmother too. I've never really thought much about her being the Queen because she's just like Granny most of the time – except when we see her on the television.'

'But how did they get her out of here?' Jacinta asked, looking around the room.

'I think it's quite likely there's a whole jumble of passageways under the house – but goodness knows how they would have known that,' Hugh sighed. 'I thought all the old maps were destroyed years ago in a fire in the east wing.'

'I don't think so, Daddy.' Alice-Miranda took her father by the hand. 'Now might be a good time for us to tell you about some of the strange things that have been going on around here this week.'

'I told you Mr Ridley was up to no good,' Jacinta smirked. 'He's behind it all.'

Hugh shook his head. 'There's no time for that now. I'm going to get Dalton. You can explain it to both of us later.' And with that Hugh raced out the door and upstairs.

Dolly slumped down onto a stool. 'I've caused a national emergency.' Her face had turned from custard to ash. 'If anything happens to her I'll never forgive myself.' She buried her head in her hands.

'It's all right, Mrs Oliver, we'll find her. Don't worry about a thing. Daddy won't let anything happen to Aunty Gee. Jacinta, can you go and find Heinrich and Mr Greening and ask them to pop down here? Millie, I think you and I should go and see if we can find Daisy and ask Granny Bert what she knows too. Mrs Oliver, you stay in case Aunty Gee reappears. If Daddy arrives before us you can let him know where we've gone. Let's meet back here in five minutes.'

Jacinta and Millie nodded firmly, and all three girls ran as fast as they could.

Chapter 36

Meanwhile, in a damp and dimly lit room somewhere on the estate, Aunty Gee was beginning to wake up. She was lying on a lumpy mattress, which smelt rather badly of mildew and old socks.

'Where am I?' She rubbed her head and removed the tiara that was sticking into the side of her skull. 'What is this ghastly place?'

The taller of the two kidnappers was standing by a thick steel door. 'Oi,' he called to his accomplice, who was on the other side of the door. 'The old bat's comin' round.'

Aunty Gee slowly sat up and shuddered at the smell which seemed to hang in every crevice.

'Where am I and who are you people?' she demanded.

'Well, I'm Bert and the bloke out there's Ernie and you're sitting here in the Palace of Versailles, and if you believe that you'll believe anything. Ain't it lovely,' the tall man snarled.

'There's no need to be vulgar,' Aunty Gee replied.

'*There's no need to be vulgar,*' he mimicked. 'Who d'you think you are? Royalty?' he sneered.

'As a matter of fact, young man, yes I am.'

The door creaked open and the shorter man, also dressed in black, joined them.

'She's a real trick this one,' the taller man laughed. 'Now sweetheart, if you wouldn't mind helping us, we'd just like the formula, that's all. You need to write it all down on this piece of paper and no funny business, awright?' He handed her a cheap notepad and a novelty pen with a fluffy troll attached to the top.

'I have no idea what you are talking about.' She pushed the pad and pen back towards her captor and rolled her eyes.

'Now listen here, lovey – either you do as you're told or someone from the big 'ouse gets it.' The shorter man ran his left forefinger across his neck. 'Maybe that little girl – she's a trick, ain't she?'

'If you are referring to Alice-Miranda, she is more than a trick and if you lay one finger on her, you will feel the full force of the law.' Aunty Gee was fast losing patience.

'Gor, you're a bit above yourself there, love,' the taller man said. Again he thrust the pad and pen into Her Majesty's hands. 'I think she's gonna be more difficult than we first thought. You'd better call the boss, Clarry. He might have to try a bit of persuasion, if you know what I mean,' he cackled.

'Shut up, you idiot – what'd you say my real name for?' the shorter man asked, screwing up his face.

'I demand that you release me this minute,' Aunty Gee commanded and stood up.

The shorter man pushed her back onto the mattress with a hefty shove.

'You can demand all you like, little lady, but until we have that formula, you're going nowhere.'

Chapter 37

In the cellar at Highton Hall the group had reformed. Heinrich and Mr Greening had been found. Dalton, the bodyguard, was pacing the room, all too aware that losing the Queen was a matter of national and international importance. Cecelia had joined them too. After noticing Alice-Miranda and Hugh's absence from the party, she had gone in search of them. When she spied Jacinta leading Heinrich and Mr Greening downstairs she realized something very strange indeed was going on.

Hugh protested that he hadn't wanted her to worry, for which he got a rather sharp telling off.

'Darling, whatever were you thinking?' Cecelia admonished. 'Aunty Gee is missing and you were going to let me continue with the party as if there was nothing wrong? She is my godmother, after all, and if anything were to happen to her – oh, I'd never forgive myself.' Cecelia sniffed, and clutched her hands together.

'Did you find Daisy?' Hugh asked his daughter and Millie as they reappeared in the doorway.

'No,' Alice-Miranda replied. 'And I'm afraid that Granny Bert wasn't making any sense at all. She said that Daisy had gone with her boyfriend. When I asked her who he was she said that he was Rupert – a lovely man – and she was looking forward to the wedding.'

Cecelia brushed a tear from her eye. 'Oh dear. I think Granny may have mixed up her medication. There was something she said to me earlier in the night – about that man with Daisy. I think she called him Mr Blunt . . . That's right, she said something about him writing a history of the Hall. Do you know anything about that, Hugh?'

Her husband shook his head.

Alice-Miranda explained that when they had seen Daisy out on the veranda earlier she looked upset. 'Golly, you don't think Daisy has anything to do with Aunty Gee's kidnapping, do you?' she wondered out loud.

'Blunt was just awful,' Millie added. 'And if he's Daisy's boyfriend, there's no telling what he might have convinced her to do.'

'Maybe *he's* in cahoots with Mr Ridley?' Jacinta surmised. 'He's up to something for sure. In fact, I saw him just now – he was outside pacing up and down the veranda talking to himself when I went to find Heinrich and Mr Greening.'

Alice-Miranda disagreed and said that she didn't think Mr Ridley had anything to do with Aunty Gee's disappearance.

For a moment silence descended on the group.

'I think we've got to find Daisy first,' Alice-Miranda decided. 'Mr Greening, why don't you take the Land Rover and head over to Rose Cottage. See if she's there.'

'All right, lass, I'll telephone if I find her.' Mr Greening nodded and left.

'Cee,' said Hugh, turning to his wife. 'Do you know of any passageways that lead from the cellar here?'

'No, darling, I heard stories about them when I was a girl, but after years of exploring I never managed to find anything,' said Cecelia, still sniffling into her handkerchief.

'All right, everyone – let's take a good look around the walls. Check for anything that looks like it could be a lever, or a latch,' Hugh instructed the group. 'They had to get her out of here somehow.'

Alice-Miranda was lost in her own thoughts. 'Plans, plans, where to find another set of plans?' she muttered under her breath as she paced up and down beside the bench. 'Oh,' she drew in a sharp breath. 'Of course!' She ran to her father.

'Daddy,' Alice-Miranda began. 'I've got an idea – I'm going to my room, but I'll be back soon.'

'All right, darling – but take the back stairs,' he replied.

'Jacinta, do you want to come with me? And Millie, can you stay here and help Daddy?' Alice-Miranda asked.

The girls nodded. Alice-Miranda and Jacinta scurried out of the cellar and then raced through the kitchen and up the back stairs towards her bedroom.

As they passed by the second floor drawing room they spied Mr Ridley. He was on bended knee talking to a life-sized bronze statue of Venus.

'Did you see that?' Jacinta puffed as Alice-Miranda pulled her along the hallway.

'What?' Alice-Miranda asked.

'Mr Ridley – did you see what was he doing?'

'Rehearsing, I suspect,' Alice-Miranda offered. 'Come on – there's no time. We've got to find Aunty Gee.'

The girls reached the bedroom and Jacinta caught her breath. 'What are we looking for up here? Shouldn't we go back and tell you father where Mr Ridley is? I'm sure he's part of all this.'

Alice-Miranda ignored Jacinta's hysterics and stood beside her doll's house. She began to take the roof apart and placed the pieces on the floor beside her.

'I don't think this is any time for us to be playing house,' Jacinta said impatiently, her hands on her hips.

'I'm not,' Alice-Miranda replied. 'Remember, the doll's house is a model of the Hall. I just thought perhaps because it's so accurate it might have the cellar too.' She continued lifting the pieces out. Soon there was a jumble on the floor.

'*Oh.* Here, I'll help.' Jacinta began removing furniture and taking the rooms apart. It didn't take long before they had demolished the upper floors.

'Look, there's the kitchen and the dining room and the sitting room – it's amazing,' Jacinta gasped.

Alice-Miranda lifted the final floor out and there before them was a maze of cellars under the house. There were even labels indicating where the tunnels headed out into the garden.

'Look – it's all there. Could you grab a piece of paper and a pen from my desk and draw a plan? Look where the tunnels are! Goodness, there's at least seven of them.'

Jacinta read out the signs. 'This one says "smokehouse", and this one says "river" and this one says "gatehouse" and this one says "walled garden" and this one says "stables" and look, this one says "Rose Cottage".'

'Maybe they haven't taken Aunty Gee very far at all!' Alice-Miranda exclaimed. 'We've got to get back downstairs and show Daddy.'

Just as the girls were about to leave the room, a voice stopped them in their tracks.

'You're not going anywhere.'

They turned around to see Mr Blunt – and this time he was sporting more than a menacing look. In his hand, pointed right at them, was a shiny silver pistol.

'*Really*, Mr Blunt – it is Mr Blunt, isn't it? – that's no way to behave,' Alice-Miranda scolded. 'I can't imagine why you would be pointing that at us. It's not very friendly at all.'

'Well, as a matter of fact,' he began, 'I'm not *trying* to be friendly, you idiotic child.'

'Now, now, there's no need for name calling. Obviously you're upset about something but waving that gun around is not going to get you very far,' she continued.

He studied Alice-Miranda as one might look at a road map written in a foreign language.

Jacinta began to cry.

'Stop that blubbering,' he demanded. 'OK – both of you – in there.' He thrust open the bathroom door and there sitting in the middle of the tiled floor was Daisy. Her hands were tied in front of her and she had a large silk scarf shoved into her mouth.

'Goodness me, Mummy won't be happy about that,' Alice-Miranda tutted. 'She loves her silk scarves and that Hermès one is a particular favourite. No offence, Daisy, but she'll have to get it dry-cleaned.'

'Shut up, Pollyanna,' Mr Blunt demanded.

'Mr Blunt, you must have me confused.' Alice-Miranda scrambled up onto the toilet lid to look him square in the eye. 'As I tried to tell you earlier, my name is Alice-Miranda Highton-Smith-Kennington-Jones and up until a few moments ago I would have been very pleased to meet you.'

'*Arghhhhhh!*' He clasped his hands to his head, obviously forgetting that he was also holding a loaded weapon. The pressure of the movement caused the gun to discharge and a bullet ricocheted loudly around the marble bathroom. All the girls could do was duck and cover their heads. *Ping, ping, ping*, the bullet shot from wall to wall to wall before glancing down off the brass light fitting and straight into the middle of Mr Blunt's foot.

'Oooowwww,' he screamed and began to leap about on one leg. Jacinta stopped crying long enough to push him into the empty bath. He landed with a thud on his head. Alice-Miranda quickly untied Daisy and pulled the scarf from her mouth.

'Here,' she instructed. 'Tie his hands and we'd better do something about that foot.' There was blood oozing through the top of his sock. 'Quick, pull his shoe off and pass me a towel, Jacinta.' Alice-Miranda leaned in and wrapped the towel around Mr Blunt's bleeding foot. 'Oh, stop that fussing,' she instructed, 'I have to put pressure on it, you silly man.'

'I'm dying,' Blunt wailed.

'No, you're not.' Alice-Miranda was very firm. 'It's just a flesh wound and I've bandaged it properly. I have very good first aid skills, sir, and I can promise that while you might experience a bit of pain, you are more likely to die from the bump on your head than that gunshot wound.'

'Oh, Alice-Miranda, thank you.' Daisy hugged her tightly. Tears ran like rivers down her cheeks. 'I'm so sorry. This is all my fault. I should have told someone about Blunt and his wicked plan. It's just that he said he'd . . . he'd kill you all if he had to,' the young woman sobbed.

'Come on.' Alice-Miranda held Daisy's hand tightly. 'We need to get back downstairs to give Daddy the details about the tunnels. Do you know where they've taken Aunty Gee?' Alice-Miranda asked.

'What? They've taken Aunty Gee?' Daisy gulped. 'I thought they must have been after Mrs Oliver.'

'I think there's been a case of mistaken identity,' Alice-Miranda replied.

Jacinta stepped back, looking satisfied. She had tied Mr Blunt's bound hands tightly to the towel rail.

Alice-Miranda locked the bathroom doors and put the key under her pillow. Just for good measure, she and Jacinta dragged chairs over and wedged them under the handles in both bedrooms that had access to the room. They would come back and see to Mr Blunt later.

'Let's go and find Aunty Gee.' Alice-Miranda led Daisy and Jacinta into the hallway.

Chapter 38

'Tell you what, you're a stubborn old cow,' the taller man grouched. 'It's funny, though – you do remind me of someone a bit. I can't think who it is.'

'The Queen?' Aunty Gee asked through gritted teeth.

'Yeah, that's it. You look a bit like the Queen. Has anyone ever told you that before?'

'Yes, they have, and that's because I *AM* THE QUEEN, you imbecile,' she roared.

'Yeah and I'm the Prime Minister,' he laughed.

Aunty Gee shook her head.

'You'd better start writing, love,' the man said, still chuckling. 'Soon as the boss gets here he won't be so friendly.'

An outer door clanged and there was the sound of a bolt sliding back into place.

A voice drifted through from the other room. 'Is she in there?'

'Yeah, and she's not being very cooperative at all. I think you might have to put some *pressure* on her – if you know what I mean.'

The inner door creaked open and a large man with a rather enormous belly entered the room. He was wearing a clown mask over his face. Through tiny eyeholes he stared at the prisoner and pressed a voice-altering device against his throat.

'Hello Dolly,' he wheezed. 'Time to get busy with the formula.' He could hardly see through the mask at all.

'What did you say?' the Queen asked.

He pressed the device to his throat again. 'I said it's time to write out the formula. You know what I'm talking about. There's someone who's very interested in FDF and they're going to pay me a lot of money for it.'

The Queen was staring at his shoes. She then looked up at his wide girth.

'What are you staring at?' he wheezed.

She stood up, took her reading glasses from her handbag and popped them onto the end of her nose. 'Percy Gisborne,' she reprimanded. 'That is the most ridiculous disguise I have ever seen.'

'I'm not Percy,' he rasped.

'And I am not Dolly Oliver, you idiot,' she snapped.

'*Oh*,' the fat man mouthed, finally taking note of who he was talking to.

'Yes, you know perfectly well who I am and if you don't stop this preposterous nonsense at once I can guarantee you will never see your allowance again,' she threatened. 'And I believe that rat-infested castle of yours was in line for some considerable renovations. Well, not any more, you cretin.'

The balance of power had turned completely. Percy made a hasty exit.

'What do you mean you're not Dolly Oliver?' the tall man asked her.

'As I told you before, I am the Queen and you had better take me back to the Hall immediately.'

In the other room, the short man was having a rather loud argument with Percy. The tall man joined them and the yelling became even more thunderous.

'You got the wrong woman, you idiots,' Percy stormed.

'We did just what you told us to. We waited until we saw her disappear downstairs and then we grabbed her. We never saw anyone come out again,' the shorter man protested.

'Yeah, I did, Clarry, but I didn't think much about it,' the taller man confessed. 'They were both wearing black.'

'You dunderhead,' Clarry ranted. 'What are we goin' to do now?'

'Get out of here, that's what we're goin' to do!' The tall man made a start for the door with Clarry on his heels.

'Get back here, you pair of numbskulls,' Lord Gisborne demanded. 'What am *I* going to do with her?' He began to weep.

In the next room, Aunty Gee studied the walls. She wondered how she had arrived in this place. The idea that there might be a secret passageway from the Hall entered her mind and she began to feel along the bricks for any unusual bumps. Her own homes had plenty of tunnels so she couldn't imagine that this one would be any different. Her hand came to rest on a loose block – she pulled on it and suddenly found herself on the other side of the wall. Inside the tunnel there was a row of rickety electric lights – most likely pre-war, she thought to herself. Aunty Gee set off through the passage as fast as she could manage in her heels. Through cobwebs and dust centuries thick she scurried on, wondering what on earth she should do about silly old Percy and his mad plan.

Chapter 39

Back at the Hall, Alice-Miranda, Jacinta and Daisy had reached the cellar. Alice-Miranda explained about Mr Blunt and his attempt to capture the girls and lock them in the bathroom.

When she told them about the gun, her mother almost fainted.

'Oh darling, you could have been hurt – or worse.' Cecelia hugged Alice-Miranda tightly.

'I don't think so,' Jacinta piped up. 'Alice-Miranda was so brave. I was bawling like a baby but she wasn't even scared.'

'That's my girl,' her father beamed.

'And Daddy, there are lots of tunnels leading out from the cellar here,' Alice-Miranda informed them.

'How do you know that?' he asked.

'Because my doll's house is such a perfect replica of the Hall, I thought that it might even have the cellar, and guess what? It does. Jacinta drew a plan.' She unfolded the piece of paper. 'Look, there are seven tunnels and they go all over the estate and even to Rose Cottage.'

'So that's why Mr Blunt was so interested in seeing the cottage and the plans,' Daisy whispered.

Through a haze of tears, Daisy managed to explain that Mr Blunt had introduced himself to her and Granny as an historian who was writing a book about the Hall. He'd had a number of meetings with Granny, who'd even found a set of old plans of the Hall in the attic to show him. But Granny enjoyed his company so much that she wouldn't let him take the plans away with him. At first Daisy had found him most charming, but she had grown suspicious after she overheard him out in the garden talking on the phone about Mrs Oliver and FDF.

'I confronted him and asked what he was really up to and he got very angry and said that if I didn't cooperate, he could make people disappear. He showed me his gun so I knew he was serious. He kept on talking about Alice-Miranda and asking me how much everyone would miss her. I was so scared I didn't know what to do,' Daisy wept.

'You poor, poor girl.' Mrs Oliver reached out to hold her hand.

'I knew zat man was up to no good. Jasper told me about zum fellow who vas poking around in ze machinery shed. I should have paid more attention,' Heinrich tutted to himself.

Daisy regained her composure and continued. 'And then I found another set of plans, for Rose Cottage and the stables and the gatehouse, so I hid them where I never thought anyone would find them – in the crisper in the fridge.'

'And I think I might have accidentally delivered them to Mr Blunt when I found them and put them on the kitchen table,' Alice-Miranda confessed. 'I thought Granny was losing her mind and putting things away in strange places.'

'Then Granny couldn't help herself and told him all about the party. He insisted on coming. I wanted to tell you but I couldn't bear the thought of what he might do,' Daisy sobbed.

Alice-Miranda put her arm around the young woman's waist. 'It's not your fault, Daisy. Mr Blunt's a brute.'

'Well, come on,' said Hugh. He strode towards the area where a tunnel supposedly linked to Rose Cottage. 'Let's see what we can find.'

Mrs Oliver looked on as the rest of the group ran their hands across the walls and searched for any sign of a passageway. Millie was crawling along the floor when her knee came down on a wobbly cobblestone. There was a loud grating noise of brick on brick and slowly a section of wall slid back to reveal a wide tunnel.

'We've found it,' the girls chorused.

Peering into the grey half-light, they could make out a figure in the distance. It was coming closer.

'I hope it's not one of Mr Blunt's associates,' whispered Mrs Oliver. She bit her lip.

Alice-Miranda squinted. 'My gosh, I think it's Aunty Gee.' She turned around to face the expectant audience, then peered back into the darkness. 'It *is* Aunty Gee!'

Alice-Miranda rushed into the tunnel. A few minutes later she emerged with the Queen by her side.

'Oh, ma'am, what a relief,' Mrs Oliver cried.

'Are you all right, Aunty Gee?' Cecelia asked and took her by the hand.

'Yes, yes, just a few cobwebs and I suspect my bunions will play up a treat tomorrow. It's quite a long way back from wherever those ghastly men took me,' she snorted.

'Did they hurt you at all, ma'am?' Dalton asked worriedly. He took her handbag and tiara.

'No. It wasn't me they were after at all. It was poor Dolly here. I hate to imagine what they might have done to you to get that formula.' Aunty Gee's lips drew into a thin line.

'Yes and I bet I know who the mastermind is.' Hugh sighed in disgust. 'I'd put my life on there being no new player with an identical formula.' He looked at Cecelia. 'I'm sure they were just bluffing until they could get their hands on our Dolly.'

Hugh didn't say so, but he was rather glad that they had taken Aunty Gee. If they'd have got their hands on Mrs Oliver, who knew what they might have done to her.

'I am so sorry, ma'am. I can't believe that they mistook me for you,' Mrs Oliver apologised.

'Oh Dolly, I can, dear. Look at us – we could be twins, and especially tonight with you in that lovely Valentino. I was rather hoping you might let me borrow it sometime,' Her Majesty smiled.

'How did you get away, Aunty Gee?' Alice-Miranda asked wide-eyed.

'Well, let's just say that Lord Percy Gisborne will be finding an alternative source of income for a very long time to come,' she replied, arching her eyebrow.

The group mouthed a synchronised silent 'Oh!'

'It appears your kidnappers were not acting alone. Alice-Miranda and Jacinta have a Mr Blunt tied up in one of the bathrooms upstairs,' Hugh explained.

'Clever girls,' Aunty Gee smiled.

'Shouldn't we call the police?' Jacinta asked.

'No dear,' Her Majesty answered. 'I think we'll deal with this ourselves.' She nodded at Hugh. 'If this gets back to the palace, I'll never enjoy another moment alone for the rest of my life.' Aunty Gee glared at Dalton who nodded like a jack-in-the-box. 'And girls,' Aunty Gee looked at Alice-Miranda,

Jacinta and Millie now, 'I know I don't have to tell you how important it is that this incident is never spoken of again. Do you understand?'

'Yes, Aunty Gee,' Alice-Miranda and Millie chorused. Millie then gave a rather wonky curtsy at which Aunty Gee couldn't help but smile.

Jacinta, however, had remained tight-lipped. The whole group turned their attention in her direction.

'Oh, all *right*,' Jacinta reluctantly agreed. 'Nothing interesting ever happens to me – and this is so much more exciting than all the silly things Mummy does – and now I can't even tell anyone!'

'No dear, you mustn't tell anyone.' Aunty Gee was stern. 'Not ever.'

'Heinrich, would you mind dealing with Blunt?' Hugh asked. 'It sounds like he may require some medical attention. Take him out the back and I'll phone through to Dr Marsh in the village. He's a confidential man. And then you can drop Blunt off at the police station and let them know you caught him breaking into the Hall.'

'The key's under my pillow,' Alice-Miranda added.

'Certainly, sir.' Heinrich grinned broadly as he left the room.

'Now.' Aunty Gee picked a cobweb from her hair. 'I think we should be getting back to the party, don't you?' She looked about at the group.

'Are you sure that's what you want to do, ma'am?' Dalton enquired.

'Yes, of course. Poor Charlotte will think we've abandoned her. And I don't know about the rest of you, but I could well do with a big piece of birthday cake.' Aunty Gee motioned for Dalton to follow her.

The group left the cellar in dribs and drabs, so as not to arouse any unnecessary suspicion. Alice-Miranda, Millie and Jacinta were the next to leave.

Hugh and Mrs Oliver lingered behind for a moment. As Hugh locked the cellar, Mrs Oliver ascended the stairs and stepped onto the veranda just in time to find Mr Greening and Lucas arriving in the jeep.

In the back of the vehicle were a couple of large wriggling sacks.

'What have you got there?' Dolly called out.

Hugh caught up and walked over to take a closer look.

'I found these two leaving Rose Cottage – they were in a bit of a hurry too, so I thought perhaps they'd like to have a chat with Sergeant Gray about what they were doing there in the first place,' Mr Greening said with a smile. 'And we can thank young Lucas here for helping me catch them.' He nodded at the boy beside him in the front seat. 'He was out for a walk when he saw me chasing these bumbling idiots. The lad's fast, that's for sure. They'd have outrun me if I'd been on my own.'

'I'll give Gray a call and tell him that you're on your way,' Hugh replied. 'Why don't you come and join us, Lucas? It sounds like you've earned yourself a piece of cake.'

'I'll be back for some of that too,' Mr Greening laughed. 'Can you ask Mrs Greening to save me a dance?'

Lucas opened the door of the jeep and walked over to Hugh.

'I believe you're Lily's nephew,' Hugh said. 'It's nice to meet you.' He offered his hand.

Lucas shook it cautiously. 'Yes, I'm Lucas.'

'Welcome to Highton Hall.' Hugh patted him on the back as they walked inside.

Chapter 40

'Where have you been?' asked Jasper, racing towards Alice-Miranda as she entered the ballroom with Millie and Jacinta close behind. 'I've been looking for you everywhere.'

'Sorry – we got caught up with something,' Alice-Miranda apologised. Millie and Jacinta exchanged innocent looks.

'I had to dance with Mum,' Jasper groaned, 'and she stepped on my toes three times.'

The ballroom was a kaleidoscope of coloured

gowns – a swirl of emerald and aubergine, lilac and buttercup.

Aunty Gee reappeared a few minutes later with Dalton by her side. He wasn't about to let her out of his sight again.

'I still can't believe it's actually her,' Millie whispered in Alice-Miranda's ear.

Alice-Miranda took a deep breath. For the first time since she had arrived home, her strange feeling had vanished completely.

Ambrose McLaughlin-McTavish interrupted the children. 'Have you seen Mrs Oliver?' he asked, his forehead wrinkled with worry.

'Yes, there was a bit of a disaster in the kitchen but I believe she'll be back any minute,' Alice-Miranda informed him.

Just as she spoke, Mrs Oliver emerged through the doorway, looking only slightly worse for wear.

'Are you all right, dear?' Ambrose asked. 'I thought you must have grown sick of my company.'

'No, not at all, just a bit of unexpected business to attend to. I am sorry Ambrose – it was frightfully rude of me to leave you all this time,' Mrs Oliver apologised.

'A problem in the kitchen?' Ambrose queried.

'Yes, something like that.'

'That's perfectly all right. Mrs Smith has been taking very good care of me.' He smiled. 'Would you care to dance?'

'Are you sure? What about your bad leg?'

'My dear, I'm expecting you to hold me up,' he chuckled.

'I'll do my best,' she said and led him to the floor.

Cecelia and Hugh had managed to slip back to the party and were taking a twirl around the dance floor.

'Do you want to dance?' Alice-Miranda asked Jasper.

'OK, but only if you keep your feet to yourself,' he agreed.

'Where has everyone been, Alice-Miranda?' Charlotte asked as she and Cyril danced past the swaying pair. 'And have you seen Lawrence? He's been missing for half an hour.'

'I'm sure he'll be back soon,' her niece giggled as Jasper attempted a fancy dip.

Millie offered to go and get some lemonade for her and Jacinta. While she was gone, Jacinta plonked down in a chair against the wall, feeling a little overwhelmed by the whole evening. She was completely lost in her own thoughts, mumbling to herself.

'Hi,' a voice spoke.

She looked up and saw Lucas standing in front of her.

'Oh, hello,' she replied. 'I'm glad you decided to come.'

'Well, I met your friend's father and he *forced* me,' Lucas replied.

For the second time that day, Jacinta couldn't help but feel that Lucas reminded her of someone. His piercing eyes seemed to look right through her. There was just something about him.

Lily caught sight of her nephew and rushed over to greet him. 'I'm so glad you changed your mind. Lawrence will be thrilled.' Lucas shifted uncomfortably from one foot to the other and scowled at his aunt.

'It's been quite a night,' Jacinta sighed.

'Yes, you could say that,' Lucas grinned.

And then, all at once, that smile – Jacinta knew exactly who he reminded her of. 'Oh!' she gasped. 'Has anyone ever told you, you look just like Lawrence Ridley?'

Lucas blushed.

'I just wish I knew what he was up to.' Jacinta scanned the ballroom, not realising she had spoken out loud. 'He was out on the veranda talking to himself earlier and then he was kneeling in front of a statue upstairs.'

'Talking to himself?' Lucas replied. 'The way you were just having your own private conversation with yourself?'

'Ha, ha,' she said and narrowed her eyes.

'I'd love to know what he was doing out there in the garden at midnight on Sunday too,' Jacinta insisted.

'Meeting my aunt, I suspect,' Lucas offered.

'Lily? But why? Does Charlotte know?' Jacinta demanded.

Millie returned with two glasses of lemonade just as Alice-Miranda and Jasper finished their dance and joined the group.

'As a matter of fact, I think she does,' Lucas replied.

'Well, I still say he's been up to no good – even if he is the most handsome man I've ever seen,' Jacinta sighed.

Alice-Miranda and Lucas shook their heads in unison.

'What were you going to tell me yesterday, at the cubby, before you changed your mind?' Jacinta asked, looking carefully at Lucas.

'Nothing really. It's just that, well, I met my father,' he replied. 'And he wants to get to know me.'

Jacinta looked as if she had swallowed a fly. 'Nothing much? Are you kidding? Well who is he?' she insisted.

'Umm . . .' Lucas glanced around the room.

'There he is.' Alice-Miranda pointed to the terrace where Lawrence Ridley was down on one knee and Aunt Charlotte was positively beaming.

'Lawrence Ridley's your father?' Jacinta's mouth gaped open.

'Yeah, weird, hey?' Lucas replied.

'But how? When did you find out?' Jacinta demanded.

'It's complicated. Maybe I'll tell you one day,' Lucas teased.

'And from the looks of what's going on out there, I suspect he might soon be my uncle too,' Alice-Miranda grinned. 'That means we'll be cousins, Lucas – how lovely!'

Lucas glanced over at her and rolled his eyes, then smiled broadly.

For the first time in a very long while Jacinta couldn't think of anything more to say.

The clock in the hallway began to strike twelve. Outside a rocket soared into the night sky, then burst into a spectacular shower of silver and blue.

'Look!' Alice-Miranda exclaimed. 'The fireworks!' She grabbed Millie's and Jasper's hands and ran out onto the terrace, with the rest of the party close behind.

And just in case you're wondering . . .

Lord Gisborne was summoned to a meeting with Aunty Gee where, in a blubbering mess, he confessed to everything. He had employed Rupert Blunt to find out all about the Hall under the guise of writing a history book. Clarry and his offsider were two idiots for hire. Along with Blunt, they were charged with breaking and entering, possession of an unlicensed firearm and fraud. The judge handed down the longest sentences on record for crimes of that nature.

Blunt claimed the buyer for the formula was Mr Addison Goldsworthy. While he couldn't prove Goldsworthy's role in the conspiracy, it seems the government had been after him for a multitude of things. He has recently been charged with massive tax fraud as well as several hundred outstanding parking tickets and is awaiting sentencing. Lord Gisborne's allowance was cut and he was forced to run nightly ghost tours of his crumbling castle to pay the bills. Aunty Gee felt that was punishment enough – for now.

Hugh signed *JAW* contracts with twenty-eight countries. Alice-Miranda decided that *Just Add Water* had a much better ring to it than FDF. Mrs Oliver has since made dazzling progress on her organic vegetable project but it's still not quite ready yet.

Ambrose McLaughlin-McTavish has given up watching television as he much prefers taking Mrs Oliver to the movies, out for dinner and on picnics. She says she hasn't had this much fun in years.

Lawrence Ridley is proving himself to be a model father. After years of not knowing he had a son, he's trying hard to make up for lost time.

For the moment Lucas is staying with Lily and her family, until some new arrangements can be made for school, but he spends every weekend with his dad and Charlotte and is helping them to plan their wedding. Alice-Miranda will soon get to be a flower girl for the third time this year.

Lucas and Lawrence share a love of choc-chip biscuits and watching re-runs of *Doctor Who*. As you can imagine, Jacinta is completely besotted – with both of them.

Lucas's mother has been home to visit a couple of times now. She wrote him a letter explaining everything. He's glad she finally told him the truth.

And it didn't take too long for Lucas to explain everything to Jacinta either. It seems that Lawrence and his mother had been married when they were very young but had quickly realized that working in movies, often in different countries, made things impossible. They agreed to go their separate ways and then his mother found out she was pregnant. Worried that a baby would hold Lawrence back in his career, she made the difficult decision to raise Lucas on her own. She said that she had planned to tell him one day, but the time just never seemed right. Lawrence became a famous movie star and it got very complicated.

Lily had always suspected that Lawrence was Lucas's father. She had argued with Kitty when the boy was born and said that Lawrence had a right to know about his son. The sisters hadn't seen each other since Lucas was a baby. But when he was expelled from school, Kitty had no choice but to ask for Lily's help. Lily agreed, but only after Kitty promised that she would write to Lawrence and tell him everything.

Millie and Jacinta stayed on at Highton Hall for the rest of the holidays. Together with Jasper, Poppy and Lucas, the children had new adventures every day but none quite as exciting as the night of Aunt Charlotte's birthday party.

And as for Alice-Miranda's surprise? Her father recently noticed that one of their three topiary horses – the old girl affectionately known as Beetle – was missing from the front lawn. Somehow she had managed to get all the way into town to Aunt Charlotte's back garden – just to remind her of home.

Cast
of
characters

The Highton-Smith-Kennington-Jones household

Alice-Miranda Highton-Smith-Kennington-Jones	Only child, seven and a half years of age
Cecelia Highton-Smith	Alice-Miranda's doting mother
Hugh Kennington-Jones	Alice-Miranda's doting father
Granny Valentina Highton-Smith	Maternal grandmother
Aunt Charlotte Highton-Smith	Cecelia's younger sister
Lawrence Ridley	Famous movie actor and Aunt Charlotte's boyfriend
Dolly Oliver	Family cook, part-time food technology scientist
Mrs Shillingsworth	Head housekeeper
Mr Harold Greening	Gardener
Mrs Maggie Greening	Mr Greening's wife
Granny Bert (Albertine Rumble)	Former housekeeper
Daisy Rumble	Granddaughter of Granny Bert, a maid at Highton Hall
Heinrich Bauer	Runs the farm at Highton Hall

Lily Bauer	Heinrich's wife
Jasper Bauer	The Bauers' nine-year-old son
Poppy Bauer	The Bauers' five-year-old daughter
Lucas Nixon	Lily's nephew
Max	Stablehand
Cyril	Helicopter pilot
Bonaparte	Alice-Miranda's pony
Shergar	Hugh's magnificent hunter
Phinnie	Family pony
Boo	Aunt Charlotte's horse
Birdy	Bell Jet Ranger Helicopter

Friends of the Highton-Smith-Kennington-Jones family

Ambrose McLaughlin-McTavish	Millie's grandfather
Aunty Gee	Granny Highton-Smith's best friend and Cecelia's godmother (among other things!)
Lord Percy Gisborne	Crusty old friend of the Highton-Smith-Kennington-Joneses'
Dr Marsh	Family doctor

Winchesterfield-Downsfordvale Academy for Proper Young Ladies staff

Miss Ophelia Grimm	Headmistress
Aldous Grump	Miss Grimm's husband
Mrs Louella Derby (nee Higgins)	Personal secretary to the headmistress
Miss Livinia Reedy	English teacher

Mr Josiah Plumpton	Science teacher
Cook (Mrs Doreen Smith)	School cook
Charlie Weatherly (Mr Charles)	Gardener

Students

Millicent Jane McLoughlin-McTavish-McNoughton-McGill	Alice-Miranda's best friend and room mate
Jacinta Headlington-Bear	Talented gymnast, school's former second best tantrum thrower and a friend of Alice-Miranda's
Alethea Goldsworthy	Ex-head prefect, school's very best tantrum thrower and enemy of most girls

Other

| Addison Goldsworthy | Alethea's father, a man of ill repute |
| Rupert Blunt | Author (among other things) |

Can't wait for more Alice-Miranda?
Read on for a sneak preview of her next adventure,
Alice-Miranda Takes the Lead

Chapter 1

Twelve pairs of eyes widened in unison, awaiting Miss Ophelia Grimm's next move. She stood in the corner of the room, a scarlet flush creeping up from her neck to her cheeks. Her blonde hair sparked with static and her lips drew tightly together.

'Out!' Her shrill voice shattered the silence. 'Get out and don't come back, you horrid little monsters!'

Eleven girls reeled backwards in terror, their hands clutching pallid faces. Millie's freckles turned white and Jacinta's mouth gaped open. Only Alice-Miranda dared to smile.

'And that, my dears, was how I got rid of the two cheeky chimps who had taken up residence in our room!' Miss Grimm smiled and plonked herself down in the striped armchair beside the fireplace in her study.

The girls exchanged quizzical looks and then disintegrated into fits of giggles. Mr Grump, who was sitting in the armchair opposite, roared with laughter.

'You should have seen those poor monkeys.' Aldous Grump grinned at his new wife. 'They didn't have a hope with Ophelia after them. Ran for their lives, they did – thought they'd be better off taking their chances with the lions out on the game reserve.'

'Very funny darling,' Miss Grimm admonished. 'I was just tired of the little brutes raiding my makeup purse, that's all. I hadn't realized chimps were fond of lipstick and blush until I caught them giving each other a makeover at the dressing table after we returned from breakfast one morning.'

Dressed casually in jeans and a pretty orange shirt, Ophelia Grimm was a picture of happiness.

'We must have stayed at the same lodge when we were on safari last year,' said Alice-Miranda, 'because the very same thing happened to Mummy. The manager, Mr Van Rensburg, said that his chimps had collected enough stolen lipstick to start their own beauty parlour. Apart from that, it does sound like you had a lovely time.'

'We most certainly did,' Mr Grump nodded.

Millie took the last sip of her hot chocolate, upended the delicate blue-and-white mug and allowed a sodden marshmallow to slide into her mouth.

'Mmm, yum!' she exclaimed.

'All done?' Miss Grimm asked.

Millie nodded.

'Well girls, I think you had better be heading off. School tomorrow and we have loads of exciting things planned for the term.' Miss Grimm stood up and walked towards the oak door.

'But can't we stay and hear more?' Jacinta grumbled. 'I want to know what happened to the baby elephant you saw on safari. Did he escape from that crocodile?'

'Next time,' Miss Grimm promised. 'And girls?' She tapped her finger to her cheek as though she had just remembered something important. 'We have a new student starting tomorrow. She'll be rooming with you, Jacinta, so I expect you to make her feel *very* welcome.' Ophelia arched her eyebrow and gave Jacinta a meaningful look.

Jacinta nodded like a jack-in-the-box.

'A new girl? That's lovely,' Alice-Miranda replied. 'I can't wait to meet her. What's her name?'

'Sloane. Sloane Sykes,' Miss Grimm replied. 'And there'll be plenty of time to meet her tomorrow. Now off you go, girls.'

Alice-Miranda was the first to stand. She said goodnight to Mr Grump, who was still sitting in his armchair. Without warning, the tiny child leaned forward and gave him a peck on his stubbly cheek.

'Now what was that for?' Aldous asked.

'Just because,' Alice-Miranda replied, before skipping over to Miss Grimm to give her a warm hug too. Miss Grimm smiled at her youngest student, with her cascading chocolate curls and eyes as big as saucers.

'And you know something?' Alice-Miranda scanned the walls either side of the door. 'I simply love your photographs. That one of you and Mr Grump is gorgeous, and that one of the elephant is too cute – you could enter it in a competition.'

The previously bare walls now played host to more than a dozen pictures – of Miss Grimm and Mr Grump's wedding, their honeymoon and even some casual shots of Miss Grimm with girls around the school. There were faces and places and memories.

'Do you remember, Miss Grimm, when I first met you I said that what this place needed was some photographs? And now look – it's perfect!'

'Yes, young lady, I certainly do recall that was one of your recommendations, among rather a few others,' Miss Grimm teased. Alice-Miranda grinned and leaned forward to give the headmistress another quick hug.

The eleven girls behind her took turns saying goodnight to Miss Grimm and Mr Grump. It was amazing how much things had changed at Winchesterfield-Downsfordvale in the past few months. Who would ever have thought that Alice-Miranda Highton-Smith-Kennington-Jones, along with eleven of her friends, would enjoy an hour in the headmistress's study, hearing all about her recent honeymoon safari to Africa?

Alice-Miranda grinned to herself. She couldn't wait to see what excitement the new term would bring.

About the author

Jacqueline Harvey has spent her working life teaching in girls' boarding schools. She doesn't have her own topiary horse in the back garden but she has come across quite a few girls who remind her a little of Alice-Miranda.

She is currently working on Alice-Miranda's next adventure.

For more about Jacqueline and Alice-Miranda, go to:

www.alicemiranda.co.uk